Zach

I would work
with you anytime.
As long as you
bring snacks.

Nat

1

THIRD LAW

LET IT BURN

by Dan Hopkins

Chapter 1.

April 2nd. Zurich. Switzerland.

Bryan Grimes sat in the steam room sucking in the moist heat, feeling it enter his lungs and sinuses. He leaned back on the cedar bench trying to relax while he readjusted the towel covering his waist. The two men who sat in the room with him were breathing deeply enjoying the heat, but Grimes was wondering when the conversation that brought them together would begin.

Grimes was a forty-nine-year-old American billionaire who had made his fortune laundering drug money for the Mexican cartels. Being subject to both DEA and FBI investigations resulted in Grimes feeling the heat and panicking, leaving the familiar comforts of America for a life on the run even though neither agency had ever issued warrants for his arrest.

Grimes' life on the run was remarkably comfortable and consisted of him not living in shady hotels or running from the police in the night, but living openly in Zurich, Switzerland in a six thousand square foot villa complete with swimming pool, steam room, six bedrooms, eight bathrooms and anything else an arrogant, flamboyant billionaire could ever want. Grimes Financial still openly operated as a legitimate business; however, secretly Bryan Grimes was a master at moving money using dummy accounts and fake corporations. He employed a small army of people around the world willing to assist him in breaking the law for a cut of the profits. Grimes' ability to launder money enabled him to continue his legitimate and illegitimate business deals in secret within the US, making and enjoying large profits and the luxuries his profits afforded him.

Grimes relaxed his toned body that he tried to keep as young as possible with his personal trainers and chefs and ran his fingers through his dyed black hair. He looked at the two men who had entered the steam room with him for a meeting that was to never have officially happened. Today's business was not about laundering drug money, but something even more dangerous and profitable for others.

The two men in the steam room with Grimes were Boris Donsky, a fifty-three-year-old Russian FSB agent whom Grimes had known for over ten years and had done business with many times in the past for immense profits, and an American named Allen Costner, whom Grimes knew very little about and always left him wanting to know more of the man. He looked like he was around forty years old, was well dressed and balding, and spoke little, only when he needed to, and with a slight southern American accent.

Boris was the first to begin the conversation for the day's business that had brought them together in secret from around the world. He spoke in his heavy Russian accent, "Have you finished moving the money to the proper accounts and is the cash ready to be disbursed?" he asked, looking at Grimes as he wiped the moisture off his face.

"It is," Grimes answered, then he began to explain. "I have set up dozens of accounts allowing access with credit and cash cards which are available now. I recommend not using them unless necessary. I have over three hundred million dollars American in cash already in the United States. The cash is completely untraceable as I used my cartel contacts; trading them laundered money for straight cash that has been circulated on the streets. I have set up the financial transactions to be made with Shura Osetsky for her purchases. When ever she needs money, I can wire it to her at a moment's noticed." Boris then looked at Costner,

"Has your boss agreed to have her husband released from prison?" he asked. Costner nodded to both men.

"Yes. He is working on the arrangements now, planning to have him placed in Russian custody if you can have the FSB ask for a prisoner exchange. That should help to avoid any red tape and keep the level of suspicion down."
Boris thought for a moment and smiled happily with Costner's answer, and then stated,

"Yes, that is a good idea. I have numerous people in custody I am sure your government would be happy to exchange him for." Costner then asked,

"Has Shura had any trouble finding the weapons we need?" Boris raised his eyebrows as though he was surprised and stated,

"No, since you had the CIA stop looking into the weapons movements, she had few problems buying and moving them. Many are already sitting in her care in multiple countries while some are at sea now. I am sure your people are happy with the weapons already delivered?" Costner smiled at Boris and stated,

"Yes, they are extremely happy. They test fired some and they may be older, but they work perfectly. They have requested more RPGs and mines if possible." Boris nodded his head.

"I will pass it on to Shura, I am sure it will not be a problem. I would have thought buying outdated, untraceable weapons would be more difficult for her, but she seems to have a talent for it."

Boris then looked at Costner again and asked, "Has your organisation been able to recruit more militia groups to its cause?" Costner smiled and replied calmly with a satisfied look on his face,

"You would be surprised how easy it is to recruit people to do illegal acts when you have unlimited amounts of cash to offer and spent millions on a compound that is the envy of every group in the country. Then add in an... attractive leader who can speak to a crowd, and it has made recruiting easy. We have only told a few of the new groups about the plan so far, but our support is building fast."

Boris nodded his head in satisfaction then said, "I must make this very clear gentlemen, and I know I have said it many times; The Russian government's involvement must be kept completely unknown. We have given you billions to set everything up and to ensure our involvement is kept secret." Both men sat silent. Grimes stood up and told the two men to follow him, he led them away from the steam room. After the three men had put on clean white thick robes, he led them into a room with a wet bar and poured them each a drink. Grimes held up his drink to toast.

"Gentlemen, to a new world of riches and power." The three gently touched glasses together and each took a swig. Grimes was looking at Costner closely, then took another drink as he placed his glass down on the bar and poured another drink as he worked up the nerve to ask a burning question, "I know I am not supposed to ask-but Costner, who do you work for? I mean, I am in this hip deep with you. I think we can trust each other, we are after all going to change the world. So, come on who?" Costner never said a word, he only smiled back while Boris laughed out loud and handed his glass back for a refill.

"Vodka please. Maybe when you see Costner here sitting in the White House beside the next president you will figure it out," he said and laughed again.

The topic was changed to a non-business genre and they began to enjoy drinks and cigars. Grimes, priding himself on being a gracious host, had some high-class women escorted into the room and music played. After some time had gone by, Grimes quickly became distracted as he was enjoying the women more than his guests, so Boris and Costner took advantage of Grimes' distracted attention and stepped outside onto the terrace for another cigar and a more private conversation. Boris looked around making sure no one could be listening, then softly said, "It is good you never say anything to him about your boss. He is good at moving money, but I feel he frightens much to easily. That is why he ran from the States before they pressed any charges. A man that panics easily the way he does can be dangerous."

Costner lit his cigar and placed the lighter back in his robe pocket and asked, "Do you have men watching him?"

Boris looked at Costner, then set his drink on the stone table beside him and tightened his robe. "Of course, I know everything he does."

Chapter 2.

April 2nd. Cedar Falls, Iowa.

Paul Totten stood devastated as he watched as they lowered his father's coffin into the grave that had been dug next to his mother's, who had past away fourteen years prior. It looked like half the town had shown up to pay their respects to his father this day. Paul's father, Patrick Totten, had been a thirty-three-year veteran of the Cedar Falls Police Department and was well respected throughout the town. Paul had rarely seen his father in the past ten years until a week and a half ago; he had avidly avoided coming home in those same ten years.

The right people said the right words about honor, duty and service and the burial was over and most of the attendees were beginning to leave. Paul continued to stand in place like stone staring where his father was now lying and feeling great regret and guilt. He felt his dad deserved much better than him for a son. He felt he had been nothing but a massive disappointment, and a source of deep embarrassment.

Paul thought back to when he was eighteen years old and he was the local high school football All-Star. The best high school linebacker Cedar Falls had ever produced. When he signed to play for Florida State the entire town celebrated with him. Less than one month into his first college season, Paul suffered a rib injury at practice and while at the hospital a blood sample was taken to check if he had any organ damage, and it resulted in finding evidence of steroid usage.

One week later he was on a bus home. But halfway back, full of shame and unable to face the town and his father, he stepped off the bus in some small backwater shithole town in the middle of nowhere and started walking. He walked lost in his mind for hours until he put out a thumb on the highway in hopes of catching a ride to anywhere. Several days later he found himself in Boston, tired and running out of money, wishing he could start over again. He phoned his dad only to find out the local newspaper had put the story on the front page calling him a cheat and the town disappointment.

Inside, he knew it was all true. He felt so ashamed after telling his father how sorry he was, and he hung up the phone and walked down the street, not sure where he was going. He walked for hours. That afternoon he passed an army recruitment center and without a thought he stepped inside and explored an option. After a brief conversation with the recruiter, it was only a few weeks later he was on his way to basic training. He did not speak to his dad for a long time, only sending him letters to let him know he was okay and where he was.

Right away Paul found that he liked the army and eighteen months later he finally found the courage to pick up the phone and call his father. He had graduated Ranger school and had once again found something he felt immense pride in. Thus, he had regained his self-confidence and joined a brotherhood he had never known before.

After two tours in Iraq and another in Afghanistan, Paul had decided to stay in the army as a career; he had found it to be a new home. Then, on a routine low-level training jump, a strong gust of wind pushed Paul off course forcing him to land in some trees, breaking his back. Two surgeries had resulted in him having several vertebra's fused together. The doctors said it was career ending, but Paul argued that he could continue to be a Ranger. He was even able to pass the necessary fitness requirements, though admittedly in great pain. Unfortunately, he was given a medical discharge with a meager pension, and then found himself lost again. At that point, he decided it was time to come home.

After ten years, he arrived in Cedar Falls. As he stepped off the bus, he immediately noticed nothing had changed except the sign that hung on the edge of town. What once proudly said for him as he left for Florida, "GOOD LUCK PAUL" was now gone. He walked down the street six blocks to the police station and stood in the doorway watching his dad standing at the coffee pot telling some young cop a war story. When Patrick saw his son standing in the doorway he broke down weeping. The two spent two good days together catching up on lost time and reconnecting their ten-year distance, until Patrick suddenly dropped dead of a stroke while sitting across the kitchen table from his son.

Paul now stood still at the grave until most of the others had left. Many were going to Patrick's favorite pub, O'Neil's, downtown for drinks and sandwiches but Paul just stood looking at the coffin.

"Hello soldier," a voice from behind him said. Paul turned his head to see Chief of Police Carter Garland walking up with his wife holding his hand. Paul immediately noticed the Chief's limp from a bullet wound to his hip years prior, which the thirty-five pounds on his stomach did not help either.

"Chief," Paul said back to him as he looked at the dress uniform the chief was wearing and found himself wishing he was wearing his own uniform, but today he was wearing a simple black suit he had just bought.

"I sure am going to miss him," the Chief said with his mouth full of chewing tobacco. He and Paul's father had been friends since they were kids and even joined the police force the same day. Paul looked at the Chief almost on the verge of tears, shaking his hand and said,

"Thanks Chief, I know how close you two were. The Chief's wife Jules was in her late fifties and was a short lady, but still had a good figure. She walked over and reached to give him a hug.

"Come here Paul," she said as she pulled him down and kissed him gently on the cheek. Paul began to tear up,

"I am so sorry I was such a disappointment for him," he said as he began choking up.

"Don't you think that boy!" the Chief replied almost angry. "Hell, the proudest he ever was of you was when you sent him the picture of you in Iraq getting that medal." Paul looked at the Chief in surprise when he heard him say that.

"I finally came home, but it was too late," Paul said, wiping the tears away. The Chief walked over and gave Paul a hug and told him to come along to O'Neil's and have a beer. Paul walked over with the couple and climbed in the back seat of their 2015 Ford Escape. As he buckled his seatbelt, he wiped more tears away.

When they arrived at O'Neil's, Paul looked at the neon blue sign and remembered when Tom, the owner, would give him a few beers as a young teenager excelling on the football field. He smiled at that fond memory as he entered the pub and found it looked the same as he remembered. The floor was covered in peanut shells and he noted the tables lining the outside walls had been updated. The bar still had the same old worn-out oak counter top and had a large picture of his father set on top.

There was standing room only in the bar and the dance floor was covered in extra tables loaded with food. Within minutes someone handed Paul a beer, which he drank down fast easing his anxiety, then had another put in his hand almost immediately. The young police officers in the department seemed to be in mourning as deeply as Paul was. They gave Paul shots as fast as he could drink them and given Paul's affinity for alcohol, he could drink them fast.

Before long, Paul was feeling the effects of the drink. Jules handed Paul a plate of food and sat with him to make sure he ate it all. She took his drink away and gave him ice water in return then told everyone not to give him anymore alcohol. She had watched him grow up and loved him like a son and tears filled her eyes as she watched him eat.

Paul was still eating his food when a short, somewhat overweight woman with a terrible hair cut and glasses walked up to him.

"Hello Paul, do you remember me?" she asked him.

Paul looked at her simply said, "Yes." The woman's name was Lana King and Paul remembered her well for she was the local newspaper reporter that that had written the article exposing his steroid usage ten years ago, after he lost his scholarship. Paul never denied the use of the steroids, but the article made him out to be the biggest fraud and embarrassment that had ever come out of Cedar Falls. She sat down across from him and said,

"I was hoping to talk to you."

"NO!" Paul replied coldly. "I have nothing to say to you!"

"Well, I know people in town would love to know what you have been up to the past ten years," she said. Paul set his fork down and looked her in the eye.

"Look Lana, my dad just passed away, this day is not about me. Please leave me alone," he said angrily.

"I understand you have been kicked out of the army," she pried, clearly trying to get a reaction. Paul was not so drunk that he couldn't tell what she was up to and he began to get angry.

"Look, bitch! I was not kicked out of the army! I broke my goddamn back!" Paul was shouting as he left the table and stormed into the bathroom and sat down in a toilet stall and began to cry. Seeing Lana made him remember the embarrassment that his father must have felt after reading the article ten years back. He sat in that dirty toilet stall until he had collected himself some time later.

Before long, people started leaving O'Neil's and heading home. Paul sat in a booth near the back wall with a couple of the young police officers and listened to them tell stories about his father. It was then Paul noticed a group of four men walk in. Paul immediately recognized two of them, Douglas Wilson and his brother Allister. The two others Paul did not know at all.

The Wilson brothers were the town troublemakers, always had been. Paul was the

15

same age as Douglas and they had never gotten along, mostly because Paul's father had arrested him several times, the first time was when Douglas was only twelve. The four men were dressed well, Paul never had seen the brothers dressed in anything that did not make them look like lumberjacks. They had both lost a pile of weight and seemed relatively fit and cleaned up good. They each had red hair which was trimmed neat, yet another thing that had changed about them and Allister had a well trimmed beard.

Paul stood up, walked over to the bar and ordered another round for the table when Douglas confidently walked over to him. "Well Paul, the local hero comes home. It has been a long-time hero," Douglas said with a heavy tone of sarcasm.

"Doug, how have you been? Oh wait... I don't give a shit!" Paul returned in the same sarcastic tone. Douglas looked at him annoyed and said in a taunting manner,

"I have been rolling, man. I have three tanning salons and two car washes. Did you see me drive up? Yea, I have a Cadillac. I heard you were like a soldier or something. What do you make a year like ten grand? Waste of a life you have." Paul looked into Douglas's eyes and suspected he was high on cocaine or something strong. Tom brought over the drinks, Paul picked them up and without saying any goodbyes, he walked back over to the party taking one of the beers off the tray, he started drinking again.

As he sat at the booth one of the officers commented that the Wilson brothers had been using their business to launder the money from the sale of weed and meth that they cultivated and manufactured in multiple hidden locations around the county. This did not surprise Paul, they had been the ones selling it back when they were in high school. Paul tried to ignore them as he attempted to converse with his father's friends. Soon the brothers and their two friends began getting loud, making sure the crowd all knew they were there. Paul looked at them again and noticed that Douglas was watching him and smiling. It was clear he was wanting to antagonize him, so Paul tried to ignore Douglas and continued drinking his beer.

"Hey, Paul!" Douglas suddenly yelled across the bar, and Paul turned and looked at him. "Your asshole old man owed me for four shitty years in the state pen! Yep, I am sure going to miss him!" Douglas, along with his brother and his two friends laughed aloud. Tom set down the beer mugs he was preparing to fill and yelled at them from behind the bar for Douglas to shut up and leave, but his demands were ignored. Paul stood up and walked over to the four men.

"Not tonight assholes!" Paul warned as the three remaining police officers who had drank too much as well stood up and backed Paul. Douglas laughed again and yelled out for the entire bar to hear,

"Three drunk pigs and an asshole never has been."

Paul looked at him calmly and said, "Jesus, Doug, why have you not grown up at all? It has been ten years!"

Douglas stared at him threateningly and said, "Yes, it has been ten years and four of those years I was in fucking prison because of your dad!"

Paul smiled back at him, shrugged his shoulders and said, "Well, fuck face."

Douglas was getting angrier and his body language showed aggression building while he clenched his fists, "It was a small amount of meth! He could have cut me a break!"

Paul began laughing, "Meth? I thought you were a pedophile!" Then Douglas lost any remaining control and swung hard at Paul's head. Paul sidestepped left while Douglas swung wildly into the air. Paul used the man's clumsiness against him and drove his knee into Douglas's ribs, driving the air out of his lungs and dropping him to his knees. Allister fought to get off his bar stool and help his brother, but Paul was ready for him and stepped closer, then kicked him in the chest knocking him and his stool over backwards onto the floor. The two friends that accompanied the brothers attempted to get in on the action, but the three young police officers dove on them both, pinning them onto the floor. Douglas was trying to make his way off the floor when the ex-ranger kicked his feet back out from under him, sending him to the floor again, this time on his back. Within a second Paul dove on top of him punching him several times in the face, feeling his nose break under his knuckles.

Allister had gotten to his feet and tackled Paul trying to pin him down. Paul twisted and turned, moving his hips into position, then reached up and drove his thumb inside Allister's mouth and made a fist, grabbing a fistful of Allister's cheek. He then quickly pulled Allister down to the right, then scissor kicked his legs, allowing him to roll over on top of Allister.

Paul began punching him, giving him an equal dose as he had given his brother. Douglas finally was able to stand, and began coming at Paul, who stood up leaving Allister unconscious and bleeding on the floor and anticipated Douglas's inevitable drunken charge. When it came, Paul sidestepped left then dropped his right foot back very quickly and brought it up and forward while rolling his hip over, striking Douglas in the side of his face with the top of his foot. Douglas dropped to the floor like a wet rag unconscious. Paul turned to check Allister and saw him still on the floor moaning and awake but holding both hands over his face with blood pouring out from under his palms. Paul then turned his body around hoping there were more; he wanted to fight more. Adrenaline filled his body, he was wild. But the fight was over and Chief Garland was standing behind him on his cell phone calling for two ambulances and a couple police

cars. He put his phone in his pocket and said,
"Jesus boy, what the Hell did they teach you?"

Chapter 3.

April 3rd. Cedar Falls, Iowa.

   Paul sat in the Cedar Falls police station cell all night. The two friends of the Wilson brothers sat in the cell beside him. They stared at the ex-ranger with fear in their eyes all night; the brothers had both spent the night in the hospital. Paul guessed it was now about eight am, he wondered if they were going to let him out any time soon and how much trouble he was in. At around nine am a uniformed police officer entered the detention room, opened the cell door and let Paul out of the cell, and walked him out to the front. His belt and shoes were returned as well as the suit jacket he had been wearing the night before. Not that it was in any condition to be worn anymore as the left sleeve had been torn half off. When he emerged to the front of the police station, Chief Garland was being lectured by his wife. Paul listened as Jules scolded her husband on making sure Paul would not be in any trouble, which made him smile to himself as he realized he would be okay.

   The officer led him to the interview room and told him to sit down, which Paul did but was wondering what this might be all about, then leaned his elbows on the table and waited. A short, chubby older man entered the room wearing an old blue sweater and grey casual pants and sat down with him. He was carrying a large briefcase which he set on the table and opened. Paul looked at him and was sure he knew the man but, could not remember who he was. "Paul, I am Franklin Murphy, your father's lawyer. Do you remember me?"

Paul thought for a second and it came back. "Yes, I do believe so, sir." Paul waited a second before asking, "How much trouble am I in, sir?"

Franklin smiled at Paul then said. "Well, none. The brothers wanted to press charges but the chief and the officers saw him swing first, so you are okay. The Chief's wife called and insisted I come down immediately and since I am here, we might as well deal with another item." He then reached into his briefcase and pulled out Patrick's last will and testament and handed it to Paul. "No surprise he left everything to you," Franklin said.

"I don't deserve anything from him," Paul said under his breath.

"Well, it is not my job to judge anyone, but I was friends with your dad for many years and I know he loved you a lot boy, so knock that off. Take you father's money that he worked hard for and saved, and do something with it."

Paul was holding back tears again then asked, "I hate to ask, but what did he leave me?" Franklin smiled politely at Paul and explained everything. To Paul's surprise his father had done very well with investing and in total, including the value of his house, Paul would receive almost three quarters of a million dollars. There was also a trust fund in Paul's name that had over eighty thousand dollars that he could have access to right away.

"I don't know what to say," Paul said.

"Come to my office tomorrow and we will get on it. Okay, son?" Franklin said, he then shook Paul's hand and then walked out.

Paul sat for a minute collecting himself, then stood up and left the room. Chief Garland was waiting in the hall and called him into his father's old office, put his hands out to the side and said, "Well, since you're here, might as well pack it up." He handed Paul a large box and together they began packing while Paul listened to the Chief lecture him on the severity of the beating he put on the two brothers and how lucky he was that neither of them were seriously hurt.

Paul opened the closet door and there was a large rifle case standing upright which Paul took by the handle, pulled it out and set it on the desk. He opened it and inside the large black polymer case he found a Remington 870 tactical shotgun and Colt M4A1 Carbine with ACOG Scope and a foregrip. The Chief told Paul that the boys on the SWAT team loved his dad and even at sixty years old entrusted with him overseeing the team, even when Patrick felt he was too old and tried to quit the team.

Paul returned to the closet and found a duffle bag. He pulled it out, opened it finding a tactical vest, duty belt loaded with magazines and equipment, a .40 Cal Glock-23. Paul knew his dad always bought his own weapons and had always said, "You want the best you have to pay for it." Paul took the radio and flashbangs off the vest and handed them to the Chief, then checked all the weapons making sure they were not loaded before placing them back into their cases. Paul looked at the wall and noticed there was a picture frame with a *Stars and Stripes* article from when Paul received his Silver Star while in Afghanistan. His eyes filled with tears once more.

After they packed the office the Chief offered to take him home and helped him pack his father's belongings out to the car. When they got to the street, one of the young officers from the bar approached Paul and handed him a newspaper. On the front page was Paul's picture, the same one on the wall from his dad's office. The article was titled, "FROM HERO TO ZERO" and told the story of Paul assaulting the brothers from the night before. It was a skewed article that made him out to be a drunken, disgruntled veteran that has destroyed everything he has touched since he was eighteen years old. Paul sighed in embarrassment and said, "Man, I can't win in this fucking town." He then told the Chief that as soon as his dad's affairs were cleared up, he would be leaving town forever.

Chapter 4.

Former Army Ranger Thomas Price had been sitting in the waiting area of the Director of the FBI's office for almost thirty minutes. Passing the time, Thomas made eyes at the Director's attractive mid-thirties Hispanic secretary, hoping she would return the smile. To his disappointment, she ignored him and continued working. "Well, worth a try," he thought to himself and lowered his gaze to his shoes.

Thomas was not alone in his wait; he was accompanied by the Director of the Central Intelligence Agency David Cromwell who was visibly nervous about their upcoming meeting.

"Nervous, sir?' Thomas asked him, knowing the answer already but he was attempting to stifle the boredom setting in.

Cromwell looked at him and smiled. "Very, I was not this nervous when Congress was going up my ass last month about the drone strikes in Colombia," he said, and he gave a small snicker.

Thomas stood up stretching his legs and back, this morning's workout was a tough one he thought. Then he walked to the doorway and looked down the hallway and noticed how everyone was dressed so nicely in this building. He looked down at his own choice of clothing. He was wearing a beige company golf shirt that had the company logo on the left breast; a black quill pen drawing the letters CIG short for Capital Intel Group. Price had worked for CIG for four years. CIG was an elite private military company and ran one of their intel operations divisions.

CIG had been employed constantly for the CIA for over ten years and had always made a point of getting the job done discretely and correctly. They had made lot of money but did not let themselves grow so big that they would have to hire substandard people who may have caused problems. CIG had kept a sturdy reputation and therefore had always been given steady work around the Middle East, developing some strong contacts in the local black markets and government agencies.

Thomas walked back to his chair and sat down again, looking at the nervous CIA Director again who was going over some notes he had in his briefcase. David Cromwell was a skinny red headed fifty-five-year-old who had graduated West Point. After his eight-year stint in army intel he had joined the CIA and became a fast climber in the agency ranks. Then three years ago, he was appointed Director. He would joke that his life turned out much easier running the agency than it would have been if he would have stayed on the family farm in Kentucky.

After another five minutes, they were escorted into the FBI Director's office and the door closed behind them. The office looked like what Thomas had expected with leather furnishing, an oak wood desk, and a picture of the President on the wall. Director Martin Bryant stood when they entered the room and Thomas was surprised at how tall the man was. At least 6'4" and damn fit for a man of fifty-six years. He was a black man born in Harlem and had worked his way though University, always demanding perfection from himself and the people around him. His suit was not overly expensive, but tailored to fit the man's body perfectly, and he kept his head clean shaven.

"David, how the hell are you?" Bryant asked to Cromwell with his deep voice.

"OH, fairly well," Cromwell replied. Both had some familiarity with each other and that would be beneficial for this meeting Thomas thought. Bryant then pointed out a woman who had just now entered the room behind them. Special Agent Reese Gilbert shook everyone's hand firmly while all the introductions were being completed. Reese was a twenty-nine-year-old blonde, five feet six and one hundred twenty pounds. She kept her hair in a tight bun and dressed in a pantsuit with comfortable shoes. Thomas looked at her thinking how pretty she was, but he was not into white women. He had always preferred the Hispanic type better. Besides, this one had a real "bitch" look about her, Thomas thought, but she was "damn good looking."

The FBI boss explained that he had asked special agent Gilbert to attend the meeting as she was one of the FBI's experts on foreign and domestic terrorist groups. Bryant thought she may have some insight on this meeting, as when the meeting was set up he was informed it was in her area of expertise.

"Well, gentleman. You said terrorists and that was all, so what is all the panic and secrecy about?" Bryant asked as he took his seat.

"First things first, everyone." Cromwell said, pulling a foil type bag out of his briefcase placing his cell phone inside it. Thomas did the same without questioning it, Bryant and Gilbert both looked at him confused and annoyed like maybe he was paranoid.

"My phone is encrypted," Bryant divulged defensively.

"Please Martin, indulge me," Cromwell asked, holding the bag out in front of him. Finally, both FBI agents followed his request and dropped their phones inside. Cromwell then sealed the specialized bag blocking all cell reception, he then sat it on the floor beside his chair.

"What is going on, David?" Bryant asked with some annoyance.

"We believe someone in the White House may be helping our enemies to send weapons and explosives into the United States. Cromwell stated this very bluntly and there was silence in the room.

"What? Care to elaborate?" Bryant asked, not believing what he was hearing.

"Let me start at the beginning," Cromwell carefully responded while Reese pulled her chair into a better position to see Cromwell speak. "Two years ago, I authorised a team to look into black market weapons movements throughout the Middle East and Eastern Europe by going after the smugglers and the ones selling to the smugglers. We got lists, lot numbers and serial numbers of the weapons that had been reported missing, or that we knew that had been sold or given to questionable groups in various countries. We then compared them to the locations we are now finding the same weapons in and patterns began to emerge. Not long after we found the patterns, we managed to bribe an informant who disclosed some names and details. We then had some good intel and we were able to pull off a "snatch and grab" on a real nasty bastard. A Ukrainian named Fedir Osetsky with ties to almost every major terrorist group on the planet, as well as East European organised crime groups. This son of a bitch provided more Russian and Warsaw pact weapons to our enemies than we could ever imagine, making more money than we could ever dream of," Cromwell explained.

"Okay," Brant said, clearly interested and wanting to hear more. Cromwell continued.

"Well, once Fedir was safely in our custody at a black site we were getting ready for some…. enhanced interrogation." He paused again and shifted in his seat. "This is where things get interesting. Somehow Martin Sibley, the Secretary of Defence of the United States of America, found out we had him and had Fedir quickly taken from us to a Federal Maximum-Security facility in Colorado, he is holding him there in protective custody. No one speaks to him... No one speaks to him at all."

"Okay," Bryant said again still sitting stone faced listening as Cromwell continued.

"Then we were ordered to shut down any further investigations in that area stating it was interfering with one of their own covert actions. He even went so far as to come into my office himself to ensure we followed his orders. As a result, we were forced to shut the investigation down. Then, within a few days of that meeting, two other arms dealers we identified were killed by who we suspect was part of the Russian FSB."

"Okay," Bryant said a third time, but his tone had changed, indicating greater interest.

Cromwell paused briefly before beginning speaking again. "I then became very concerned as some of the weapons were heading to ports off the coast of West Africa, which sends a lot of goods Stateside."

Bryant placed both hands on the desk top and pushed back in annoyance, and in disbelief blurted, "Wait, are you telling me the Secretary of Defense has personally interfered in an investigation that allowed weapons to be smuggled inside the United States?"

"Yes, I am," Cromwell stated confidently.

"This is crazy!" Bryant shouted in outrage. Cromwell matched the volume and tone of his counterpart.

"Just wait, listen some more. I will let Mr. Price explain the rest."

Thomas Price stood up nervously, he opened the briefcase he had brought with him pulling out some files. He handed them to Bryant and Reese while clearing his throat before he began to speak, "Sir, I work for Capital Intel Group, I am not sure sir if you have heard of us?" He pointed to the CIG logo on his shirt and waited for a response. Bryant said nothing and shrugged his shoulders. Thomas continued his briefing, "Our training center and office is only twenty-six miles east of Washington. We have done a lot of contract work for the CIA and other agencies over the past few years and are known for our discretion; we have developed a good working relationship with the Agency. Some time ago we were approached to carry on the investigation that Mr. Cromwell was ordered to shut down in secret. Using copies of the files that Mr. Cromwell's people gathered, we began looking around. You see sir, CIG has developed many good contacts around the Middle East, especially in the black market and the intel communities. It was necessary for some of the work we had been asked to carry out in the past. It was very easy for us to find out that Fedir Ostseky's wife, Shura, she had carried on with his business as efficiently as he had after he was grabbed by the good guys." Bryant was looking angry and Thomas figured he had better get to the point. "Sir, in the files in front of you is a list of weapons we have confirmed are in shipment right now to the United States. All these weapons are listed as being stolen from former Warsaw nations or known to have been given to countries known to support terrorist or to the groups themselves." Bryant was still angry but, listening, so Thomas went on. "The crate numbers from Interpol's files you will see sir, were matched to the shipments being moved by Shura Osetsky by one of our contacts in Libya. Another set of numbers was confirmed in Bosnia."

Bryant looked at the files. The look of annoyance on his face had been replaced with interest. "If you look at the weapons lists you can see, Sir, they are all older weapons, and I believe are listed to have been taken out of some nations illegally. That would keep a certain vodka drinking country's hands clean. Most of the weapons are hand held, shoulder fired stuff, sir. RPGs, SA-7s, explosives and mines, AKs and the types of weapons an insurgent force would need to start a major action in this country. I had my guys take out a few of these supply caches, one in Morocco was headed to a sea port, another in Turkey that was to be loaded on a ship headed towards Newfoundland, Canada."

Reese who had remained silent was looking at some photos in the file that she was provided with great interest. Her body language changed as though she suddenly remembered something and looked to her boss and impatiently asked, "Sir, may I run to my office? I would like to grab a file I was working on earlier this morning, I think it may have some bearing on this case." Bryant nodded to her and she left the office almost running while Bryant took the time to ask Cromwell how his son was doing this year in college. A few minutes later she returned with a file in her hands and sat down thumbing through it until she found the page she was looking for. Pulling it out, she held it in one hand and checked the file Thomas had given her. Thomas could see she was looking at lot and serial numbers. "Shit, sir, we may have a problem." Reese said with some shock on her face and looked again at the file while everyone in the room watched her with great interest waiting for an explanation. "Three weeks ago, an ATF team raided a farm in Illinois. The farm was owned by the head of True Brothers of Illinois. They are a real radical group screaming for armed insurgency and are suspected in the killing of a state trooper. After the raid the ATF found a cache of weapons, RPG's and explosives. These numbers on this file Thomas provided match with the lot numbers on the crates found in Illinois. Also, there was a large amount of cash found on the farm, more that the True Brothers of Illinois could raise in a life time," Reese explained. There was silence in the room. Bryant looked at Reese and asked with his deep voice. "Do you have any idea who these idiots in Illinois have relationships with?" Reese looked at her file again and finding some information and answered.

"They have friends all over the country through social media and rally meetings. They get together, shoot guns and drink beer. Tell each other how tough they are but really that is all most of the time. But we know one group in Michigan called the MLB, the Michigan Light Brigade, led by a hardcore lunatic named Isaack Elsey whom we know has been meeting with True Brothers a lot the past few months. We suspected they formed some sort of an alliance. The MLB has been spreading money around and uniting groups together under Elsey. The money they have been spreading around is more than they should ever have had the ability to access. Their support in their local community is strong, they have been recruiting men and women as fast as they can. They have a compound outside of Flint that is impressive to say the least." She finished speaking and all four present in the room said nothing for a moment.

Thomas waited a moment before he spoke. "Mr. Bryant, sir. I have concerns that the Secretary of Defense is assisting Shura Osetsky in sending weapons to the United States and possibly arming domestic insurgent groups." Silence filled the room again. No one spoke until Bryant asked a question to the group.

"Do you guys know where Martin Sibley is from? I mean where he was born and raised?" There was silence in the room one again until Bryant spoke.

"Flint fucking Michigan." He slowly said again, while the silence continued.

"What do we do now?" Reese asked.

Thomas lifted a hand and stated. "We need to send someone inside the MLB. Someone known to be disgruntled with the government and who has something to offer a militaristic group."

Cromwell raised his hands and stated, "CIA is out, I am sure we are being watched. That is why I hired CIG."

Bryant then shifted uncomfortably in his chair and said, "I will bet my pension that we are surely being watched too then."

Thomas raised his hand again and said, "Well, what about us? CIG has something more to offer in this."

Cromwell looked at Thomas and wondered what he was talking about. Bryant looking interested again and asked. "Like who? You sound like you have something in mind."

Thomas smiled, reached into his briefcase and pulled out an article he printed off the Internet that very morning, "I do Sir, I have found this newspaper article online earlier this morning, I printed it off and tossed it in my briefcase to read it later. Funny how I found it this morning and needed it now. I served with this guy, and trust me sir, I know him, he is perfect and no ties to the CIG,

35

FBI or CIA. He can pull off being a disgruntled vet easily. Through dozens of missions and raids we covered each others asses in the Rangers countless times, and if things go bad he can take care of himself." Thomas said, handing the article to Bryant.

Bryant looked at the article title and dropped his head to his left side when he read the title out loud. "From Hero to Zero."

Chapter 5.

April 15. Cedar Falls, Iowa.

Paul had been busy cleaning out the garage at his father's house, taking another load of the forty years of collected junk away to the city dump. He had taken most of it that morning and this was his last load, but this was going to be placed into storage. There were some things he just could not part with yet.

He had not been feeling any better about his father's passing, so he worked constantly, trying to bury the deep hatred he had for himself. The real-estate agent had recently placed a For Sale sign on the lawn of his father's house and Paul could not wait until he could leave this town forever.

The newspaper article "From Hero to Zero" played heavy on his mind as though it was torturing him. He had read it a dozen times and each time it stung worse. Lana had almost encouraged the entire town to think of him a drunken embarrassment to every resident of Cedar Falls. Every time he left the house, people would stare, point and snicker behind his back.

He also had no idea of where he could go; most of his friends were still in the Rangers and those that had left the army were spread out all over the country. Paul felt as lost and alone as he had when he had gotten kicked out of school ten years prior.He placed the last of the contents of the garage in his father's 2006 Ford F-150 and was just about to head to the storage lot when a taxi pulled into the yard. Paul watched to see who it was. When the rear door swung open a man stepped out who Paul instantly recognized.

"Tommy!" Paul yelled at his old friend as he jumped out of the truck and trotted over. "Seeing a buddy is something I need these days, man. God, what are you doing here anyway?" Paul delivered excitedly, seeing Thomas had instantly brought some life back to him again.

"I came to see you buddy." Thomas replied then asked, "Got a moment to talk?"

"Of course, hop in, you can help me unload this stuff." Paul said, pointing at the truck. They jumped in and headed to the storage yard where Paul had rented a locker to hold anything he wanted to keep from the house he grew up in. Thomas' intended business had not come up yet, as they spoke about mutual friends while catching up on the Ranger gossip and spoke of their time in the military together.

After they finished unloading the truck's contents into the storage locker, they jumped back in and Paul began driving them back to his house. When they were leaving the storage yard Paul signaled for a left turn, but Thomas said, "No, go to the right." Paul looked at him and asked, "Okay, why?" as he made the right turn.

"Head to the town airstrip. I have something to show you." Thomas said.

"What are you being so vague about, man?" Paul asked his friend confused.

"You will see!" Thomas replied with a knowing smirk. The drive to the airstrip took about fifteen minutes from the storage lot. Thomas showed him where to park and they walked to a pilot who was waiting near the edge of the parking lot. After brief introductions he escorted them onto the runway where walking a impressive private jet awaited them.

Paul started laughing, "What the hell, buddy?" Thomas laughed with him and said, "Come on cheese dick get on the plane! I have something to show you and I promise I will have you home by midnight." They followed the pilot onto the Legacy 600 private aircraft sporting the CIG logo on the tail.

The plane took off almost immediately and when they were in the air, Thomas got up, walked to the fridge and grabbed two cold beers. He handed one to Paul and they both opened them at the same time and each took a drink. Paul looked at the inside of the plane taking in the leather couches, chairs and the polished wooden table in the middle. "Damn nice buddy! Contracting pays well I see. Or are you selling crack?"

Thomas took another drink and smiled at his buddy. "It is not mine, it belongs to CIG." Thomas said.

"I figured," Paul replied then added. "So, does CIG always allow their employees to spend company resources to take a buddy on a joy ride, to relax and have a beer?" Paul asked.

"It is not like that my friend, I will explain everything when we get to CIG HQ. So, for now enjoy the flight and let's drink some beer. God damn, it is good to see you," Thomas said with a grin. Paul wondered what this was all about, guessing he was being recruited. He began to feel like he was going to let his friend down as he thought of his back injury.

"Look buddy, we have been through some shit together and I will always have your back forever, anytime. But you know I trashed my back, right? So, I don't think CIG management will accept my resume. Thanks for thinking of me, but it is a waste of time." Thomas laughed out loud.

"Dude, would you relax. Enjoy the flight and drink more beer, it is free!" The flight was not long only a few hours, if that, when they landed at the small airstrip in Edgewater, Maryland.

When they exited the plane, a small helicopter was waiting for them. An all black UH-6 Little Bird skipped over and landed to pick them up. Paul and Thomas sat on the crew bench on the outside of the Little Bird and Thomas signaled the pilot to take off. The ride to Davidsonville, Maryland took only minutes as the fast bird skipped along the treetops at high speed. Paul felt a familiar rush of adrenaline and remembered how much he had missed this, especially when engaging insurgent fighters from a bird just like this one, there was no way Paul could feel anything but exhilaration. "Good times." Paul shouted aloud, smiling as this brought back good memories.

They landed a few miles outside of Davidsonville at the CIG headquarters building on a small makeshift helipad pad big enough for six Little Birds, which were all parked sitting idle. Paul climbed off the helicopter and walked towards the hanger feeling like a soldier again. The CIG facility was large, containing five small chopper hangers, and three warehouses which Paul guessed were twenty thousand square feet each.

They walked past a large shop that had the hanger door open where it looked like men were armoring some vehicles. The office building was two stories tall and looked more like a lawyer's office than a private military contractor's headquarters. The entire facility was fenced off with a small security guard shack watching over the front entrance. They even had a kill house off in the distance and some men were standing around getting ready to practice breaching. Paul recognized more than a few of them from his time in the Rangers. Paul smiled, "Impressive, you have recruited half our old unit here." He stood in one place, turning in circles taking it all in, then looked back at the men getting ready to enter the kill house. To his surprise, he recognized another member of the team and asked Thomas, "Hey, is that... Is that fucking Tim?" Paul immediately left Thomas's side and headed for the men at the kill house laughing the entire way. Once he got closer he did recognize one of the men as Tim O'Brien. "Holy shit!" Paul yelled out and the group turned their attention to him, "Are things so tough for this outfit that they have to recruit north of the border?" Paul shouted out laughing. Tim O'Brien looked at Paul and began laughing,

"They just realized they needed some high-class operators down here, so they made me an offer I could not refuse," then held up his finger and thumb and rubbed them together giving the universal sign of cash. Paul and Tim walked towards each other laughing and gave each other a big hug.

Tim O'Brien was a Canadian who had spent years in the Canadian army's elite special forces the JTF 2. Some years back he was sent down to Fort Benning as an exchange program training with the Rangers and ended up deploying into Afghanistan with Paul and Thomas's unit. Tim was a fit six feet tall, and two hundred pounds. He had brown hair and spoke with a very slight lisp.

At first everyone was skeptical of the foreigner from the great white north being attached to their Ranger unit until they realized he really knew his business, and not to mention was one of the best shots in the world. O'Brien was with Paul when Paul won his Silver Star and had earned some chest candy himself that day. "What the hell are you doing here? Are you coming to work?" Tim asked Paul, excited.

"I don't know, maybe." Paul answered his friend.
They stood chatting for several minutes, Paul was
greeted affectionately by the other men in the unit
that he had previously served with. Thomas's cell
phone alerted him he had received a text. He took
a quick glance and said.
"Come on buddy they are waiting," and they
started walking towards the office building.
"Who is waiting?" Paul asked. Thomas said nothing
and just kept walking-leading Paul through the
front doors and up a flight of stairs, then down a
hallway that lead them into a large board room.

Two men wearing CIG shirts sat quietly in the
back, and two men in suits sat at the large oval
table. Paul noticed a very beautiful blonde in a
pantsuit sitting at the table with the other two but
had the look of someone who looked way too
uptight, but he took a second and third look at her
and felt immediately attracted to her. The
boardroom had several large video screens on the
walls and a communication station with several
computers. Paul realized it could double as a
situation room if needed.
Thomas told Paul to have a seat and then some
introductions were made around the table. Paul
was blown away that he was in a room with both
directors of the CIA and FBI. He shook hands with
the female FBI agent named Reese who smelled
amazing. The two men sitting back who belonged
to CIG, judging by their golf shirts said nothing.
They were introduced as the owners of CIG and

just watched while taking notes. At this point, everyone's cell phones were collected then safely sealed in a foil bag and even then, the bag was taken out of the room.

Paul leaned forward nervously placing his elbows on the table as he began to listen to everyone tell the tale of the illegal weapons movements, and how they were coming into the country then being distributed. They chose to leave out the part about the White House and the Secretary of Defense in case he was found out and pumped for information. After they finished briefing Paul, no one said anything as they gave Paul a moment to process it.

"The fuckers!" Paul broke the silence with a shout as the anger filled his body. "These inbred militia guys here at home are trying to turn New York into a shithole like Baghdad! Have you been to Baghdad? I have... it sucks!" Paul finished his rant when he noticed everyone staring at him and he realized how unprofessional he must have sounded. "Sorry, what do you want from me?" Paul asked.

Thomas turned his body in his chair to face Paul, and prepared to divulge the plan,

"Well buddy, we want to send you into the Michigan Light Brigade as a recruit and find out everything you can."

Paul started laughing. "Really? Have you lost your mind? I am not trained for this shit." Paul said disbelievingly.

"You are perfect," Director Cromwell spoke out. "You were an Army Ranger, a damn good one from what I hear, one of the best. Which would make the MLB desire you. Your history of being kicked out of the NCAA for taking steroids, your release from the military is well documented on your file, and you fought the medical release. You have a real reason to be bitter at this nation, and finally this is the icing on the cake," Cromwell opened a folder and tossed him the newspaper article "From Hero to Zero." Paul face turned red when he saw it.

"So, you guys read that?" Paul said embarrassed. Director Bryant then spoke up.

"It makes it all fit nicely. Your life story can be found on the Internet, so we want to send you in as yourself. Tell them the truth about everything, except, you know, leave out us," Bryant explained. Thomas stood and walked around to the other side of the room, turned to face Paul and said, "We need your help buddy and you will be paid well." Paul looked at everyone as they waited for him to respond. "Well, I have nothing else to do," Paul said, as several people in the room let out a sigh of relief. "Is there a cool code name for the mission?" Paul asked as his excitement was starting to show. The directors and everyone looked at each other wondering themselves. Cromwell was the first to speak up,

"We are sending you against a power force, like Newton's third law, for every action, there is an equal and opposite reaction. How is operation Third Law?" No one in the room said anything and all sat content. Paul nodded his head, liking the code name for the mission and slowly said out loud, "Third law."

Chapter 6.

April 27. Flint, Michigan.

Paul had finished setting up his bedroom in the small apartment he had found in city of Flint, Michigan. He had been in town three days, moving there shortly after he had completed his father's affairs. The house had been put on the market and Paul had zero intention of ever returning to Cedar Falls again. Paul placed his father's weapons and tac vest in the closet of his new apartment and shut the door. "I need a proper gun safe is what I need." Paul said aloud to himself. He then looked for and found a good hiding place for an encrypted cell phone he was given to contact only Thomas or Reese. He wrapped it in plastic then pressed it inside a block of butter and simply put it in the fridge.

Reese was living in Flint as well, she had taken an equally small apartment just down the street. He looked at the flyer on the kitchen counter, then to his watch and realized he would be needing to leave soon. The MLB were having a recruitment rally tonight at a farm just outside of town. Paul picked up the flyer again and gave it another read. "Bring the family, free food and games for the kids. Isaack Elsey will be speaking, NRA members welcome, freedom from oppression is coming," was all written around the MLB logo of a man holding his hands over his head while breaking the chains he was bound in.

"Very dramatic," Paul thought as he finished his pizza then quickly drank a bottle of water and left his apartment.

He emerged onto the street outside and looked in the direction of Reese's apartment wondering if he should let her know he was going to the rally tonight. He decided not to tell her.
She had a bad habit of talking condescendingly to him like he was a child and that pissed him off. "I am a decorated Army Ranger and a combat veteran, she needs to learn to shut her mouth and show me some respect! To bad she is so damn good looking," he thought as he climbed into his dad's old pickup.

He closed the door and drove to the outside of town following the directions on the back of the flyer. The closer he got, the more nervous he became, he could feel his stomach was getting upset. "I should have brought my gun," he said to himself. He found the lane-way to the farm and pulled off the main road as the darkness of night was beginning to set in. Paul drove inside the gate where a young teenage boy dressed in a plad shirt and bluejeans directed him to park in the field. "Just find a place in front of one of the sticks with a ribbon, okay?" The young farm kid directed. Paul followed his instructions, but then decided to park near the back of the several hundred vehicles already there.

He got out of the truck and walked towards the sound of a large crowd talking, laughing and mingling. He made his way through a patch of trees and could not believe what he saw, it looked more like a circus than a radical recruitment rally. Four bouncy castles were provided for the kids. A small stage was placed near them with a sign letting everyone know country music would be played after Isaack was done speaking later in the evening. Numerous flags waved in the air featuring the MLB logo alongside the American flag. Paul walked around a large barn that was open; he passed people who walked out holding cold beers, or drinks for the kids. Paul walked inside and it was packed. He estimated with the kids and people outside there was close to six hundred people present here.

He pushed his way to the bar. It was nothing more than plywood sitting on tin barrels. He asked for a beer. A bottle was placed in his hand with a smile from the toothless hillbilly who Paul found incredibly creepy tending the makeshift bar. "Dental Plan!" Paul thought to himself as he took his first sip of beer, then walked over to the left side of the barn where people were picking up plates and dishing themselves up generous portions from a terrific looking spread laid out on the tables. Paul did the same, piling his plate high and then moved outside. Numerous picnic tables had been placed around the area and Paul found a suitable spot sitting himself down and began eating some of the most delicious fried chicken and green beans he had ever had.

"Is it good?" A female in her late forties asked as she walked over, giving herself permission to sit down across from Paul, while opening a beer.

"Yes, this chicken is better than my mom's and the beans are amazing," Paul answered while wiping his mouth.

"The chicken is mine," she said proudly. Paul smiled at her while he took another bite. She had a real farmer's wife look about. She was short, a little heavy, with short brown hair and a real pleasantness about her. "Where are you from? I haven't seen you before," she took another sip of her beer.

"Iowa." Paul said. "I just moved here a few days ago, found the flyer and thought maybe I would check it out. I checked out the website, this Isaack guy seems to know his business."

"Yes, he does. My name is Kelly, Kelly Alderman," she said holding out her hand.

"Paul Totten." He replied and shook her hand. "Well Paul, what brings a young man like you from Iowa to Flint?" she asked. Paul got the feeling that she was interrogating him and he had only been here sixty minutes. "Just out of the army, no family, no friends except those still serving. I could not stay in Cedar Falls and couldn't wait to leave, so I just woke up, threw a dart at a map and came here for a clean start I guess," Paul explained.

"Army?" she asked.

"Yes, Rangers, ten years, then I broke my back in a training jump and they released me, but I am fine, but they wouldn't listen. They took the only home I had left," Paul explained.

"You're a sweetie," Kelly said, smiling at him as she got up and left the table. Paul watched her walk away and thought about how nice she was.

A little while later Paul had just finished eating and was placing his paper plate in the trash hoping to get another beer, when an older man who was tall, skinny, white-haired, with a large grey mustache and smoking a cigarette, walked proudly onto the stage. He took the mic off the stand and turned it on.

"Hello there!" he yelled, and the entire crowd cheered for him. "I guess most of you know me, and for those who don't, well, I am Isaack Elsey. General of the Michigan Light Brigade." The crowd cheered him again. Paul left his seat and grabbed another beer, but returned as fast as he could to hear the General speak.

Isaack began his speech talking about his wife Sarah and what a wonderful mother she had been to their child before he sadly passed from a treatable ailment, but the proper healthcare that the child needed could not be obtained. Isaack spoke of how he and his wife were unable to afford the needed medical treatments and it was not his failure, but the nation's failure and how wrong the country was for allowing it all to fall apart. Paul watched the crowd as they ate up every word Isaack spoke.

He then began speaking of the corrupt federal government and how the individual states being cowardly and corrupt themselves to stand up to the federal monster slowly forcing them into slavery. He spoke of unfair taxes; that a hardworking man cannot keep what he has worked so hard for. He spoke of high unemployment and the government spending billions by bringing in millions of colored people, giving them good jobs because they are willing to work cheaper, therefore making the rich even richer all the while destroying the middle class and their way of life. A way of life their fathers had fought for. He spoke of the CIA allowing the nation's children to be corrupted by creating the drug trade to make money, then using that money to start unjust wars that kill the future of our nation.

Paul listened and found himself silently agreeing with some of Isaack's logic. He spoke of the United Nations steadily gaining power, secretly being run by a group of the richest people on the planet with their end game of a one world order. Of the hundreds of people in attendance, most were eating it all up.

"Isaack is one hell of a speaker." Paul thought to himself. Paul continued to listen and watch the crowd get more excited. It did not take long before the talk began turning to violence and armed insurrection which made the people cheer him on even more.

"There are people like us all over this nation!

They need leadership and unity!" he yelled making them cheer louder. He believed that it would only take one single grand action against the government to cause their brothers and sisters to finally rise and join them in the fight. He went on and on for almost an hour before saying his goodbyes. Before leaving the stage, he introduced the band and told everyone to enjoy the free drinks and barbeque.

Paul went back into the barn retrieving himself another beer, while men and women walked around handing out application cards for the MLB with pencils to fill them out. Paul took off his coat and draped it over his right shoulder making sure his Ranger tattoo on his left upper arm was clearly visible. "Rangers Death Before Dishonor" written on a ribbon wrapped around a dagger was Paul's choice years back. He had seen many others after that he liked more than his and always regretted not being more patient, but the work was good, and it always got him the attention he wanted on the beach. That and the bullet hole on his left thigh made for a good story for the ladies.

Paul made his way to the outside wall and drank his beer. Before long the tattoo had been noticed by many in the barn and people were talking about him. He stood leaning against the wall with his beer and as he expected, a five foot eleven, stocky, unshaven man wearing a desert camo operator's cap walked up to him and handed him another beer. "Rangers, huh?" the man asked him.

"Yep," Paul replied to him.

"You deploy any place?" The stocky man asked.

"Three tours; one in Afghanistan, two in Iraq," Paul said.

The stranger looked at Paul and asked the question. "You kill anyone?"

Paul looked at him not answering as he put his hand out to the man. "Paul Totten."

The man grabbed it hard and gave it a shake. "Timothy Jones. Lt. in the MLB," he said proudly.

Paul looked at him and sarcastically asked, "Really, have you killed anyone?"

Jones gave Paul a strange look then snickered and slapped him on the back, "Come on Ranger! Have a shot of Bourbon with me." Paul followed Jones over to the makeshift bar where each man had a single shot of Bourbon, Paul thought the burn felt good as it went down his throat. Grabbing another beer each they stepped outside and sat down. Timothy Jones began asking the same questions that Kelly had asked him earlier, and after Paul answered them again, Jones handed him a recruitment card. "Hey, want to join the MLB? We could always use someone who knows how to fight, I mean we got lots of vets but guys with your experience are rare." Paul began filling out the card. He began putting in his personal information, it even had a spot for references. Jones continued grilling Paul all night long by asking him about where he grew up, his high school, he even went so far as to verify Paul's story with a quick Google search on his smart phone. "Holy shit man! You got drafted by Florida State?" Jones shouted.

"Yea keep reading and see how great that worked out for me," Paul said back sarcastically. He had stopped drinking beer and switched to bottled water. He had to drive home after all.

Jones began laughing loudly. "Shit man, steroids! You fucked up a full ride and all that free pussy in Florida." Paul silently looked at Jones and shrugged his shoulders. "Crazy shit man! Say tell you what, do you know where the MLB compound is?" Jones asked.

"Nope, new in town remember," Paul answered. "Okay, so just keep driving east down this road about ten miles and you will see the guard towers on the right," Jones explained.

"Okay, why?" Paul asked him.

"Tomorrow at two pm be at the compound and make sure you bring your guns, we are going shooting." Jones excitedly said.

"Alright then." Paul agreed to his invitation, then stood up, shook Jones's hand firmly and then explained he was tired then fashionably left. He made his way back to his truck, he figured it was better not to overstay his welcome on his first day.

The drive home was uneventful. When he parked outside his apartment it was past one in the morning. To his surprise, Reese was waiting outside parked in her car.

"Get in!" she ordered angrily.

"What?" Paul asked.

"Get in!" she ordered again. Paul walked around her car and got in on the passenger side. As soon as he shut the door, she started the car and drove away.

"Yes?" Paul asked with a sarcastic tone.
"Where the hell have you been?" she yelled at him, clearly pissed off.
"Doing what they are paying me for! Holy shit lady! Calm down!" Paul said back in the same tone as she had attacked him with.

"I asked you a question!" she shouted. Paul reached into his pocket pulling out the flyer advertising the rally and handed it to her. "You went to this event without telling me?" she shouted,
her anger was now much worse, and she pulled the car over into an empty parking lot. "Are you really trying to get yourself killed?" she shouted again.

"Oh, for crying out loud, calm down! I can take care of myself!" Paul shouted, beginning to lose his composure.

"Don't tell me to calm down! I am responsible for you! I need to know where you are at all times!" she snapped.

"Okay, fine! I am way too fucking tired to argue, just take me fucking home!" Paul shouted almost in her face, Reese sat there looking at him creating a very uncomfortable silence.

Reese started to calm down and said, "Paul, if you go to something like that again, I need to know. If something goes wrong, I need to have people nearby to pull you out if needed." Paul said nothing, he just looked out the window. After another minute of silence, she regretfully said, "I am sorry. These people are dangerous and I knew you were doing something like this. I could feel it and I was worried you might get hurt. Paul, you are not trained for this kind of work." Paul then looked at her and nodded his head at her. "So, what did you learn?" she asked curiously.

Paul explained the night to her in detail; as she listened, Reese was very impressed with how much detail he could remember. He told her about the speech Isaack made in detail with the affect it had on the variety of people in the crowd, and the high numbers of attendees at the meeting.
After he was done she asked him to write a report for her and drop it in the trash can behind his apartment tomorrow evening for pickup. She started the car and began driving him home. Paul looked at her in the darkness and could not believe how attractive she was. Her skin was perfect, and her eyes were hypnotizing. It had been a very long time since Paul had been with a woman. His back injury had made it difficult to have sex for some time and since then, well the opportunity had not presented itself. When Reese was not angry and patronizing him, Paul felt it hard not to make a move on her.

They pulled in behind Paul's apartment building. As Paul was going to get out Reese began to ask him another question about his father. Before long the two were speaking to each other like friends and soon they were laughing. After another thirty minutes past, Paul said he had to get some sleep and then remembered something. "Oh, I forgot to tell you. I am going to the MLB compound tomorrow at fourteen hundred. That guy Timothy Jones I told you about invited me, were going to shoot some shit." Paul told her.

Reese began getting angry again but, caught herself and simply said, "Okay." Paul smiled at her as he climbed out and walked into his apartment and wondered how long it would be before he had the chance to get her in bed.

Chapter 7.

April 28. Flint, Michigan.

   The next afternoon Paul grabbed a coffee while making the drive to the MLB compound outside of Flint. He timed his arrival to be exactly 13:55 hours as being too early would mean he was too excited and being late would mean he didn't give a shit, so Paul had decided to play this cool. He drove off the highway at the turnoff when he could see the guard tower off to the right just like Jones had said. The road leading up to the compound was in good shape and the guard towers were visible from a long way off. Paul followed it in and stopped in a gravel parking lot outside a fenced off area. It looked more like he had pulled up to a state prison than an extremist compound.

   Paul stepped out of the truck grabbing his duffel and rifle case that had been his dad's only a few weeks past. He began walking towards a building that was built into the fence that contained a two-gated vehicle entrance allowing for vehicles to be searched in a contained area. Razor wire sat on the top of the ten-foot-tall fences. As he walked up to the small building he looked over at the closest guard tower; he could see a man wearing the old-style tiger striped camo and holding a scoped AR-15. He stood watching Paul closely. The entire place was covered in cameras, he noticed one camera followed him as he walked to the gate house.

He pulled on the door, but it was locked. He stepped back wondering if there was a doorbell, but then the door let off a loud click and a buzz which signaled him to pull, but he did not pull it fast enough and it locked again. He tried pulling the door again, but it was locked, and he stood feeling a bit embarrassed waiting for it to buzz once more. Finally, it buzzed again, Paul pulled the door which allowed him to enter the gate house and stood at a large counter. Behind it was a large young man wearing the same tiger striped camo and was wearing a holstered Colt 1911 on his hip. He walked up towards Paul and politely asked,

"Can I help you?" Paul looked the large young man who was maybe twenty-five, he had to be six foot one, a solid two hundred thirty pounds of pure muscle. Paul looked at him closely and thought the guy must live in the gym. He could sense the young man had a real anger inside him. His blonde head was shaved into a mohawk and both forearms were covered in bad tattoo work.

"Yes, I am here to see Timothy Jones, he invited me to go shooting. My name is Paul Totten." Paul said as politely as he could. The young man stepped away from counter, picked up a phone, and made a call. Paul took the time to look around the room again and noticed an x-ray machine and metal detectors. The room also had four cameras placed all around it.

After the young man hung up the phone, he walked back to the counter.

"Okay, Mr. Totten we need to screen your bags. Please place them on the x-ray machine and we will run them through." Paul did as he was told. The young man turned on the machine and stood at a screen watching closely as Paul's gear moved through.

"Nice toys, Sir," The young man said as the polymer case ran through the machine and he noticed the rifle inside. When Paul's bag came out the other side the young man asked him to open it. Something inside had given him some concern. Paul unzipped the bag and was told to take everything out.

Paul began removing everything from the bag. The first thing he pulled out was his father's old tac vest. Paul had rearranged it for his liking, but he purposely left the police issue patches on it. The young man saw the police patch and got very excited. "What the fuck is this?" He yelled, as he held up the tac vest and pointed at Paul's father's old police patch.

"A Velcro police patch." Paul said, getting the reaction from the young man he was hoping for. Paul had purposely left the patch on the tac vest to let them know he had kept no secrets from them.

He realized that it may be a risk and expected it may cause confrontation, but he thought about it and decided to leave it on hoping to tell them the story of his father recently dying and that he had left them on to honour him.

Maybe it would help his back-story and a little sympathy never hurt.

"I can fucking see that! Are you some kind of fucking pig?" The large young man yelled in Paul's face.

"No, wait," Paul calmly said trying to explain but was cut off.

"We do not allow pigs in here! You need to leave... now!" Paul looked at the young man who was red-faced angry. He was hoping for a reaction when the patches were noticed, but this kid was losing it.

"It was my father's vest. He was a cop in Cedar Falls. I leave it on out of respect for him, that is all, I meant no disrespect. I will remove it now, I am sorry," Paul explained apologetically, then pulled the Velcro patch off the vest and tucked it in the bag.

"I told you to leave... pig!" The enraged young man screamed, breathing heavy as adrenaline squirted through his veins.

Paul began to realize his idea of showing the police patch was a complete disaster, most people it would have worked on, but this buffoon was raging so bad Paul suspected him to be on something. "Probably the steroids." Paul thought, as he admitted to himself that his plan was completely idiotic and so was he for trying something so stupid at an important meeting such as this.

"Look I am sorry, I am not a cop, I was only released from the army less than two months ago," Paul calmly said, trying to reason with the enraged bodybuilder. The young man placed his hand on the Colt at his side as a stern and quiet threat.

"I said leave, pig! You are trespassing!" Paul realized how badly he had messed things up. He was not going to get anywhere with this buffoon. He realized he would have to leave and maybe try getting in touch with Jones another way. He picked up his bag and weapons case and was about to head for the front door when the back door leading to the compound opened and Jones walked in carrying a large thick folder.

"Hey, you are leaving?" Jones called across the room.

"I was hoping not to," Paul said then pointed at the large enraged gorilla staring at him red-faced. "I pissed him off," Paul explained.

"Alfred," Jones said as though he was talking to a child. "Did you hurt my new friend's feelings?" Again, speaking to him like he was a child. Alfred reached over the counter, took Paul's bag out of his hand and reached inside. He pulled out the police patch and showed it to Jones.

"He's a fucking pig!" Alfred shouted. Jones looked at the patch then then at Paul and calmly asked.

"Well, are you a goddamn cop?" Jones asked calmly while looking Paul in the eyes. Paul explained the story of his father and the how he had left the vest the same for sentimental reasons.

Jones looked into the file he was carrying, then pulled Alfred to the back of the room and had a quiet conversation. Jones handed Alfred the file he was carrying and opened it to a page. For nearly five minutes, Alfred read some pages in the file and Paul began to wonder if the steroid freak could even read-it took him so long.

Finally, Alfred finished reading and handed the file back to Jones but continued shaking his head. Jones began to reason and ended up poking Alfred in the chest giving him a stern lecture until he finally consented, though with much hesitation, and waved Paul through the metal detector. Of course, it beeped. Paul reached into his pocket and pulled out his truck keys, some loose change, phone and a small collapsible knife with a locking four-inch blade. He walked through again without any problems. He reached for his belongings and Alfred grabbed his phone before he could pick it up. "Phones stay here!" He placed it in a lockbox and handed Paul the key. Paul knew better than to say anything else as he was afraid he may antagonize the boy.

"Sorry about the mix up," Paul said as Jones lead him into the compound while Alfred looked at him like he was Satan himself.

Paul walked into the compound following Jones and looked around trying to take in every detail he possibly could. Two old raised roof red barns stood close to the front of the compound. One housed some horses, Paul could see them looking out the stalls as the front door was wide open. The other he could tell had had some renovations completed in the past. It had several satellite dishes on the roof with some radio antenna's as well, he could see reinforced doors and caged windows. There were numerous vehicles parked around the main gate and barns.

Jones lead Paul to a four-seater John Deere Gator. He told Paul to toss his gear in the back; Paul then climbed in the front passenger seat and they drove deeper into the compound. "How much land do you guys have here anyway?" Paul asked as he continued looking around noticing more cameras facing outside and inside covering much of the compound.

"Oh, about thirteen hundred and eighty acres, but only one hundred sixty is fenced." Jones detailed.

"Really, you have a hundred and sixty acres fenced and is it all covered with cameras?" Paul asked surprised.

"Camera's and towers, man. We have towers every two hundred yards all with search lights and camera feeds, landline phones and radios my friend." Jones explained.

"Holy shit," Paul said astonished, then asked, "Must have cost a fortune. Did Isaack win the Powerball or something?"

Jones laughed out loud as he drove the Gator faster down the well-groomed gravel road, "Nope, let's just say we have faraway friends with deep pockets. If you think what you have seen so far is good check this out." They rounded a corner through some trees and came out into another clearing. What he saw impressed him even more. Hundreds of large solar panels were laid out in perfect lines. The wires lead into a large green tin cladded building which was also connected to a large wind turbine that stood slowly spinning beside it. Fifty yards further
they had a vehicle park with eight school buses of various sizes, several Kenworth trucks with long trailers and a few dozen Winnebago's of different models and years.

"Holy shit dude," Paul said smiling.

"Yep, and we're not done yet." A moment later Paul detected the faint smell of sewage in the air and he saw a large mobile home park with at least thirty trailers laid out in three circles, complete with a children's playground and baseball field. Jones looked at him and smiled. "Yep, we have a permanent residence here of over a hundred people inside the compound, not including Isaack up at the big house over there," he said pointing at a large new two-story farm house with a covered deck running around all four sides.

"I had no idea man," Paul said in disbelief as he noticed they were driving towards the big house. "Where are we going?" Paul asked.

"Isaack likes to look into the eye of every potential recruit himself," Jones told him. They pulled up to the house and were greeted by two armed guards all wearing the tiger striped camo. They greeted Jones and Paul in a friendly manner, then told them Isaack was waiting out back. But first they removed the knife from Paul and searched him for anything else he may be hiding on his body. After the search was completed, and one of the guards had grabbed Paul's nuts, they walked up on the porch and followed it around the house. Jones had the file he had shown Alfred at the main gate in his hand.

As they rounded the house to the back, Isaak was sitting drinking coffee having a cigarette at a table with four chairs. He saw them coming and stood with the cigarette in his mouth, he shook Paul's hand then told them both to sit down. His wife Sarah hurried out and poured coffee for the newcomers, then went back inside leaving sugar and cream. Jones sat down first and handed Isaack the file, then gave Isaack a quick thumb up.

"So, you were a Ranger I hear," Isaack said, not asking, but stating.

"Yes, sir," Paul said, feeling nervous in front of this man as he had a hard look about him. Isaack looked through the file, flipping through some pages.

"Shit son, you seen some action," Isaack said.

"Yes, sir, some," Paul answered.

"Had some trouble when you were young, had some trouble when you were in the army and recently too," Isaack noted.

"Not really trouble, sir." Paul said, feeling the need to defend himself. Isaack sat the folder down on the table and left it open. Paul glanced at it quickly as Isaack opened a fresh pack of smokes grabbed another cigarette and lit it. He then set his lighter down on top of the pack, Paul noticed the shine of the silver lighter and a small strange bird like symbol engraved on the lighter, but thought nothing of it.

"You have a copy of my military file?" Paul asked, very surprised. There is no way he should be able to have access to that Paul thought.

"I do. We have friends in terrific places, son. Now back to the trouble in the army," Isaack asked him sternly and clearly wanted Paul to tell the story, so Paul obliged him.

"Sir, I would not call it trouble either, sir. I broke my back on a jump after I hit some trees. After a few surgeries, I was still able to pass the fitness standard, but the army still said it was career ending and punted me out. I fought the dismissal but one officer, a major who was a real bean counter, policy slave, with no honour, would not listen. I may have made a bit of a scene at the hearing that ended my career."

Isaack listened to Paul as he explained getting red-faced. "So, after three tours, getting shot in the leg and having a good friend die in my arms; the prick says, "Goodbye son, enjoy your pension!" So, I grabbed his coffee mug that said something about keeping your honour and I smashed out a window in the boardroom. I mean, they let people who are missing limbs stay in so why could I not? I loved the army, I really did sir, and it was taken from me." Paul finished his rant and it seemed to satisfy Isaack.

"Now, let's get down to business. Why do you, the son of a cop, want to join the MLB?" Isaack asked while looking Paul hard in the eyes.

"To belong, sir," Paul said.

"Bullshit!" Isaack said. "If you lie again you will be escorted off the compound!" Paul looked at him hard, wondering what to say. Reese and everyone said to him to not lie, just tell the truth, so that is what Paul decided to do.

"Okay, when I was eighteen years old I was a great football player, got a full NCAA ride. The ride was cut short when I was found to be on steroids. Yes, sir, I was cheating and I am sure you know this already." Isaack nodded at him and Paul continued. "I was so humiliated because back home in Cedar Falls the local newspaper attacked me and embarrassed my father, so I decided to join the army to avoid going home. Before long I realized I loved the army. I made Rangers; you know this, you have my file. You know I did three tours and saw three tours of bullshit politics that did nothing but got good people killed so the rich could get richer." Isaack was still watching him closely as

Paul continued, "Then I came home and got hurt in a training jump and they said take your pension and leave boy, but they forgot about my honor, sir. I went home to the only thing I had left, my dad, then he died two days later sitting across the table from me. The entire town turned on me again with the bullshit newspaper article about the bar fight, so I left again and ended up in Flint. I saw your flyer which directed me to checked out your website. It got me thinking and goddamn if it did not make sense to me!" Paul found himself with his voice raising as he got somewhat excited again. "That is when I came to see you speak last night and found myself drawn to your words, sir."

Isaack watched Paul's eyes as he told his story not looking away for a second.

"We need men like you Paul," Isaack said softly. "What if it does come to violence?" Isaack asked him carefully.

"Everything in my life has turned its back on me. I have no loyalty left for anything in my past." Isaack looked at Paul as he took another drag on his cigarette.

"Tell you what Paul Totten," Isaack said slowly. "You can start helping out around here for a while to see how you like it. First, I will ask you to start training some of my men in small unit tactics on a probationary period," Isaack offered.

"I am not one to brag, sir, but that is right up my alley, I will straighten them out," Paul said calmly.

"Excellent! Jones take this man to the range and see if he can shoot."

"Yes sir," Jones said. They walked back to the Gator and drove away heading towards the firing range.

Chapter 8.

May 10th. Washington D.C. The White House.

Secretary of Defense, Martin Sibley, gave a smile to the President's secretary, and a quick knock on the door before walking into the oval office at the request of President Sterling Hunton. "Good afternoon Martin, sit down please. Want a coffee?" The President asked.

"Sure, I could use a strong cup," Martin replied to the Commander in Chief as he watched him press a button on the phone, then speaking to his secretary politely asking her to bring coffee for Martin and himself.

Martin watched his boss and could not help but strongly hate the man. Everything the President had accomplished in his entire life had come so easily for him. Even the physical look of the man was impressive. He was naturally fit, good looking and recently even at fifty-seven years old was voted as one of the sexiest men in America. He was famous for his perfect brown hair, that the more it turned grey the better it looked. His square jaw and blue eyes made him seem like a super hero and his wife, Tracy, was the perfect First Lady and the nation adored her. The couple even had a son in the Marines who was wounded in Afghanistan, which helped him secure his victory in the election. Everything had always seemed to work out in his favor.

Even after all that, the biggest thing that Martin hated about his boss was the way the man could speak. When he gave a speech, the man could work a crowd into frenzy or bring them to tears, even both in the same speech. His popularity with his legitimate, nice guy reputation made Martin sick to his stomach with envy, and he hated everything about him, especially many of his foreign policies.

Every time Martin was with Hunton he would end up trying to compare himself. Martin's hair was grey, and he always had to fight to keep it neat. His body turned everything into body fat which made him have to spend hours a week on the treadmill to keep in shape. Martin had an impressive career himself, but it never held a candle to Hunton's. Harvard Law degree, City of Detroit DA, a Michigan state senator, and the ambassador to Russia, but nothing mattered because Hunton was the President of the United States and Martin could not stand him for it.

Moments later the coffee was delivered on a platter set on the table in the middle of the room. The President's secretary placed four sugars and double cream into Martin's, stirred and handed it to him. She poured the President his coffee and left the room. "What can I do for you Mr. President?" Martin asked.

"Hey, it's just us buddy, so cut out that Mr. President bullshit," Hunton said to him.

"Okay, Sterling," Martin said softly and took a drink of his overly sweet coffee.

"Did you read the brief from Eastern Europe this morning? The goddamn Russians are beefing up on the borders again. I have had calls from both Georgia and Latvia's ambassadors this morning asking for help. The Ukrainians are almost beating down the White House front door screaming for more assistance," Sterling explained and waited for Martin to verbalize his thoughts.

"Ahh, that is just Russian arrogance. They are trying to scare everyone again, so we won't bring in the sanctions you have threatened them with," Martin explained, like the Russian aggression was of little concern. "Besides, NATO is moving troops into the area and the Russians know it. I know President Shuisky. He is not crazy; aggressive yes, but not crazy. He knows better."

Sterling took a drink of his coffee and stated softly, "The Georgians have asked us to take one of their new air bases near Oni, crew it up to help and deter the Russians in the area. I think we should take their offer; the base is up and ready to go. We could have planes and crew in there from Germany in days," Sterling suggested. Martin was getting frustrated but did his best to keep his emotions hidden. Martin tried to reason.

"Sir, moving more assets into the area could raise tensions."

"Or lower them," Sterling said sternly back that initiated a silence as both men sat and took a sip of their coffees.

"Look Martin, I know you know the Russians better than anyone. Christ, that is the reason I asked you to be on my team to help me with the new Russian threat. But I am sorry, we will be moving planes into Georgia from Germany as soon as possible." Martin took another drink and sat the empty cup down on the tray.

"Well I guess it can't hurt. I will talk to the generals and get the ball rolling, sir," he said as he stood up. "I better get on it," Martin said and began walking out. "Thank you, Martin," the President said to him and it was returned with a nod.

Martin walked down the long hallway to his office trying to hide the frustration on his face. He walked past his secretary's desk and told her to hold any calls, then motioned at one of his aides who was sitting in an adjoining office to come into his. Allen Costner followed him in and shut the door behind him. As soon as the door closed Martin let out a growl and slammed his fist down on his desk top trying not to scream in frustration. "I hate that man more than anything!" Martin blurted out. "The son of a bitch has ordered me to send planes into Georgia from Germany." Costner looked at Martin without any surprise on his face.

"Does not surprise me, Shuisky is very impatient. He knows the time is coming and sometimes gets impetuous. I will contact Boris and see if he can get him to pull back some of his troops and calm things down," Costner said.

Martin walked across his office to his small bar and poured himself a drink and added some ice. He then walked to his desk and loosened his tie after he sat down. "How are the weapons deliveries going?" Martin asked Costner as softly as he could manage his rage.

"Good. Though two shipments have been destroyed overseas, we are not sure by who, but they were easily replaced. Isaack says the recruitment is going well, he has added a few hundred more to his numbers by bringing in some more groups from several other states. The money is helping greatly with the recruiting." Martin took a drink and sat silently thinking.

"Two shipments taken out? Do you think it was Langley?" Costner shook his head.

"No sir. They think it was probably the Brits or the French. Both have been looking at black market weapons shipments hard lately, trying to keep them out of their own backyards away from the Muslim threats they have. We are clean, sir."

"Excellent, when might the "Act" happen?" Martin asked. Costner thought for a second, then answered.

"Well, the weapons are coming in steadily, but we need to stockpile more of them first. Then they need to be stashed in other states as well with some friendly groups. That will take some time, but if all goes well ten months, maybe eleven Isaack thinks." Martin listened to Costner closely and took a sip of his drink then gave Costner an angry look and quietly said. "When we do this...the act. Tell Isaack, I want Sterling dead!"

Chapter 9.

May 11. Flint, Michigan.

Paul reached into the fifty-gallon plastic barrel of ice water and felt around until he found a cold beer, then walked over with his plate to receive a large portion of barbequed ribs before finding a place to sit down. The event organizers provided long tables and benches for the one hundred plus men and women who Paul and a few other veteran members of the MLB had been training most of the day. He had worked them hard today and everyone felt they had earned this meal.

Paul began eating the ribs and baked potatoes; after the first bite he thought he had died and gone to Heaven. The ribs were unbelievably good. "Why do you folks want to takeover the country with violence? You could conquer the entire nation with this barbeque," Paul said aloud as he took another large bite of the ribs, causing an uproar of laughter at the table.

He had been training members of the MLB three to five days a week since they had first asked him to apply, he was beginning to get to know many of them. After every day of training Paul would go home to his tiny apartment, where he would make notes of the day's activities inside the compound and any additional intel he may have gathered. After his notes were completed, he would then toss them in the trash bin outside the apartment allowing them to be retrieved later that night by

Reese. Sometimes he would exit the apartment out the back, taking a walk for a mile or two through alleyways or going for a run, to make sure he was not being watched. Then he would meet Reese at her apartment, which was located just down the street where she would debrief him face to face.

Paul had noticed more than once that he had been followed by someone who he suspected was an MLB member while he was taking his daily run, so he simply just gave himself a good workout and returned home. Isaack was a careful man and his screening processes for new recruits was thorough and tough. The MLB kept Paul's duties to the firing range and other areas of training, making sure he would see nothing illegal. Everything around him was legal; the weapons, vehicles, everything he saw inside the compound was legitimate. He knew this would change in the future, he just needed to prove his loyalty and in the meantime, he would continue to report member's identifications and building layouts to Reese nightly.

One thing Paul did notice was a strong undertone of racism in many of the members which made Paul very uncomfortable. The more members began to open up to Paul, the more they began talking openly to each other of their hatred towards black and Latino people. All too often Paul had a hard time holding his tongue. Some of the filth certain members would openly talk about disgusted Paul, especially the trash that came out of Alfred's mouth. Alfred Johnson was, in Paul's mind, a complete asshole and Paul hated him more than anyone he had ever met in his entire life. "Well maybe there is a certain reporter bitch in Cedar Falls that might top Alfred on the list," Paul thought to himself.

Kelly Alderman walked over with another beer handing it to Paul, then sat down across the table with her own plate and began eating. "Can I join you?" she asked Paul after she had a mouthful already,

"Of course," he replied, then took a long drink of his beer. Kelly was wearing the tiger striped camo that every MLB member wore. Paul had not been given any to wear yet, so he chose to wear his old Ranger military issue battle dress uniform with a new pair of jungle boots he had bought in town. He completed his outfit with a Ranger t-shirt and desert camo operator cap. "How are the ribs?" Kelly asked him.

"Oh, my God Kelly, they are so good," Paul said as he took another bite. Kelly smiled at Paul and began eating.

"It was a good day today," Kelly stated like she was proud of her day's work on the training field.

Paul looked at her then replied. "Kelly, you are a hard worker, you would have made a good soldier." She looked at him and began talking, her voice had changed as she added a hint of sadness in her tone.

"Did I ever tell you about my son, he was a solider. Did you know that?"

"No," Paul replied, she looked at him and took another drink of her beer before speaking again.

"He was a soldier too. He joined the army right out of high school, never saying a word to me about it until he had already signed up. We could not afford to send him to college after we lost everything in the 2008 financial meltdown, so he said if he served, the army would help him out." Paul watched her tell the story and could see she was getting emotional and right away Paul knew how this story was going to end. She continued her story and it was beginning to sound like a confession. "He completed his training and was almost immediately sent to Iraq, he sent me letters letting me know he was safe and that he liked his job. But when he would phone I could hear in his voice how unhappy he was. He was killed protecting a convoy loaded full of air conditioners meant for some oil executive's offices." Tears filled her eyes and she choked out another sentence. "My son died, so some millionaire assholes could sit in comfort and get richer." She took another drink of her beer. Paul said nothing and just sat with his hands on the table looking at her and waited for her to collect herself.

"I am sorry," Paul broke the silence with Kelly who said nothing, she just reached across the table and held Paul's hand for several more minutes as she collected herself before returning to her meal.

Paul watched her for a moment in silence as it all made sense why a sweet lady like her was with this group. He would have to talk to Reese about helping her when they all get arrested in the near future.

Moments later, Alfred's voice could be herd from a few tables over, breaking Kelly's concentration on her sorrow as she looked over at him. "He has been drinking hard with his buffoon friends again," she stated while shaking her head, then began to eat again. Paul looked over at Alfred and his group of drunk, young immature friends and like Kelly, he simply shook his head.

Alfred had it in his mind that he was a real Spec ops level warrior, but after several training sessions Paul realized that Alfred was just plain stupid. He could shoot some and was in good physical shape but was unable to work as part of a team in any function. Paul especially noticed it during the team training scenarios he would run; Alfred would just start yelling at his team even if someone else was the designated team leader and usually ended up calling a childish version of a charge. Alfred would charge ahead of the team alone, then end the scenario by proudly saying, "Always do what the enemy least expects," or something ridiculous like that, and Paul was really getting tired of him. He found his presence during training very distracting as the man just would not shut up.

Isaack stood behind one of the grills, turning the meat as it sizzled and smoking a cigarette as usual, greeting people as they came by for a helping. Paul finished his ribs and went for seconds, it was a long day and he needed to "feed the machine" as he liked to tell Kelly, as he left the table asking her to hold his spot. Paul walked up to Isaack and asked for ribs, Isaack smiled when he saw the ex-Ranger standing in front of him. "Well soldier, how are you fitting in?" Isaack inquired.

"Not bad," Paul answered looking Isaack in the eye. "You have many great people here." Isaack nodded his head, then handed Paul a large rack of ribs and said,

"Folks around here like you boy, and the training you have been providing has been terrific. Hell, even some of our vets say it's top notch." Paul made eye contact with Isaack and grinned.

"Well, sir, I am glad to help out. Also, like I said, you have good people here," Paul stated to the general, then walked away making his way back to Kelly, until he suddenly saw Timothy Jones walking towards Isaack with an unknown white male. The strange man had a shaved bald head and a tattoo on his neck. Paul stopped and grabbed a few more potatoes and tried to see if he could hear something. Jones and the unknown man walked up to Isaack and Paul heard Jones quietly say,
"Vlad showed up at the gate. Needs to speak to you in private." Isaack handed the tongs to another man standing nearby and told him not to

overcook the ribs, then the three of them walked away. Paul watched and waited as the three walked off into the darkness. When they were far enough away he discretely set his plate down and followed, but not in the same direction. He headed in the direction of the portable toilets Isaack had provided for the day's event. He went inside quickly urinated giving more time for his discrete exit, then left the toilet, but instead of heading back to his meal, he stepped behind the toilets into the darkness heading towards Isaack and the other two.

Isaack stood in a grove of trees thirty yards from the barbeque. Paul quietly moved around the grove to the opposite side. He ducked down and slowly moved into the trees to hopefully find a spot where he could hear them speaking. He moved slowly, staying low until he could make out a voice. Paul stopped moving and closed his eyes, slowed his breathing into long slow breaths, while he strained his ears to hear. After a moment, his senses became more focused, something that had been sharpened from his time in the army. He began to make out Isaack's voice asking about a time schedule. He then made out another man's voice with an east European accent say "Next Sunday and then again Monday night, meet the boat at the same time and location. You will need two trucks the same size as the last time. Don't be late!" Then Paul made out the sounds of a movement as the three were heading back to the barbeque. Paul waited for several moments and made his way back the same way he came in.

After Paul made a discrete re-entry into the party, he picked up his plate and headed back to his table. As he passed by Alfred's table of drunken friends, Alfred saw Paul walking passed and then leaned over whispering something to his friends and a snicker ran over them all. Paul looked at Alfred and smiled, thinking how immature he was, as he passed by. Alfred noticed Paul's smile and quickly jumped up, instantly enraged. "Hey! What the hell was that?" He yelled at Paul who stopped and turned around holding his plate. Paul noticed that everyone at the barbeque had stopped eating and was now watching them. Paul, did not want any trouble, but was having a tough time holding his tongue. He said to the raging young man,

"Alfred, this is not the time for you to start. People had a long day and are enjoying themselves, so let's not mess up the night." Paul then turned his back and casually walking away.

He was walking along one of the large tables towards Kelly who was patiently waiting for him to return. She saw him coming and smiled at him, but the smile instantly left her face as something big and heavy hit him in the back driving him to the ground. Paul was flat on his face on the ground trying to catch his breath as Alfred stood over him laughing.

"Smirk at me now loser!" Alfred shouted as he pointed down at Paul like he was in the ring at an entertainment wrestling event. Paul rolled over and looked up at Alfred. He stood up and faced the raging bull. "Well boy, where is your smirk?" Alfred yelled again. Paul looked around and could see the entire crowd had stopped eating and drinking and just sat stone faced watching. Paul was never one to take shit from anyone. He finally caught his breath and looked at Alfred.

"What the hell is wrong with you? Did you find that necessary?" Paul asked him.

Alfred laughed and simply said while drunkenly laughing. "Yes!"

Paul looked at Alfred again and responded. "Alfred, this is something I know something about. Steroids make you stupid."

Alfred started to say something, but Paul quickly stepped forward and gave Alfred a quick, straight left jab directly onto the end of his nose, causing his head to snap back. Paul took advantage and stepped in again grabbing him by the back of the head and pulling it forward and down. At the same time Paul brought his knee up high striking the enraged boy in the face, sending him to the ground landing on his ass in shock. Paul took two steps back and looked at Alfred's friends sitting at the table who were all still sitting watching with fear on their faces. Alfred sat on the ground trying to get the blood out of his eyes while cursing at Paul, who was standing waiting for him to climb to his feet. A second later Kelly grabbed Paul and pulled him away, another second passed, and Jones was standing in front of Alfred giving him a lecture about steroids and alcohol abuse. As Paul walked away he looked back and saw Isaack watching him closely and he wondered if maybe he had screwed up his chances with the MLB.

Chapter 10.

May 12th Moscow, Russia.

Boris Donsky walked into the Russian President False Shuisky's office and closed the door behind him before he said a word. President Shuisky waited for the sound of the bolt to catch before he excitedly shouted to his old and most trusted friend. "Boris, you old pig fornicator, how are you?" Boris gave a loud laugh and returned,

"Well, probably as good as you, you son of an Afghan goat." Both laughed aloud with each other as they took hold of each others' wrists and shook while False had not yet left his chair. President False Shuisky had known Boris since they had served in Afghanistan together many years prior. False raised his fifty-nine-year old, overweight body out of his chair and walked over to the many varieties of alcohol he had laid out on a two-hundred-year-old wooden table that stood under a large window in his office.

False was a well-known alcoholic, and a bad one at that, the skin around his nose was bright red to the point it looked almost painful. False let out a grunt as his lower back let him feel his age with a small spasm causing him a brief moment of pain. He poured drinks for both he and Boris, then brought them back to the desk, and handed one to his friend, then let himself drop back into his chair and he let out a sigh of relief. Before any more conversation False complained of his bad back like his friend had no idea he was having troubles.

Boris listened to the complaining, then laughingly reminded him of that day in Afghanistan when False took the shrapnel and how it was he who carried his former commander out of that ambush and ending the tale with, "I don't think I could do it anymore. You have put on too much weight." False looked at Boris and replied almost defensively.

"We have both gotten too fat, my friend. Life has been good to us."

"Yes, it has," Boris agreed. False smiled at his friend and said,

"It is good to see you my friend. It does my heart good." Boris grinned, happy to hear the compliment and stated back,

"We should make a point of visiting more, don't you think?"

"Yes, we should," False replied. They spent a few minutes catching up on personal details, reassuring each other that they would always be there for one another for life.

"Okay, let's get the business talk out of the way before we drink to much and make no sense at all," Boris said to his boss who laughed and agreed.

"How are the different stages of the plan moving?" False asked.

"Very good. We have a few small problems that need ironing out, but with your help they can be easily taken care of," Boris explained. False shrugged his shoulders and said,

"Well, let's deal with those first then." Boris leaned forward and began speaking.

"Great, first order is the matter of Fedir Osetsky. He is being held in the United States, in a maximum-security facility and we require an official offer of exchange for him for someone the Americans would be willing to trade him for. His wife Shura is becoming impatient on the matter. I have prepared a list of suitable candidates for your consideration, please," Boris explained and handed over the list to False, who glanced at it and nodded his head in approval. "Also, I received a message from Costner. He has stated that Georgia is allowing one of their new airbases to be turned over to the Americans and President Hunton is publicly stating he is combating our so called, aggressive actions toward the region. He has given orders to have planes flown into those bases within the next two days. Costner is recommending we draw back off the borders to deescalate the tensions until they have the time to place the plan into motion. Then we will have less American influence in the area to deal with." Boris was careful in the tone he used, making sure False was not going to fly into a rage. False took another drink and simply agreed with Boris.

"It will be done," False said calmly.

"How much longer before the American terrorists commence their attack?" False asked his friend. Boris looked at him, thinking.

"Isaack is hoping for the attack to start in less that ten months. Then Eastern Europe will be ours for the taking again my friend," Boris explained to his friend who grinned happily, then stood up and headed to the table to refill his drink.

"For what it has cost us, it had better work," False muttered, almost making it sound like a threat.

"I have never let you down False," Boris stated, and his boss acted like he had never heard him say it. False walked back over and sat the bottle down beside Boris's glass in case his friend needed a refill. Boris then calmly said to his boss,

"Everything will workout False, trust me, America will begin to burn itself into a failed state within a year. Then with the Yankees trying to clean up their own house, no one will be able to stop us from taking back what was once ours, or anything else we want." False thought for a moment, then quietly muttered to Boris, "Anything else I want?"

Chapter 11.

May 13th Flint, Michigan.

Paul returned to his apartment from the MLB compound dirty and tired. Apparently, after Paul's altercation with Alfred, Isaack was not mad at him at all. In fact, Paul got the odd feeling it may have even strengthened his position with them. Isaack had asked for him to be brought to the house. He asked Paul how he was for money and how he lived without a job. Paul had expected this topic to come up sooner or later. Paul asked Isaack to bring him to a computer, then logged into his pension website and bank account. He was able to show Isaack to the penny how much money he was bringing in every month. He also showed Alfred his bank account and told him of the money his father had left him in the trust. Paul explained to him he knew that he would have to find some work some day, but just wanted to take some time off and adjust to civilian life after a decade in the military. Isaack seemed to have bought Paul's story because it was, in fact was all true. Isaack's mood changed to a lighter tone and he told Paul how much he appreciated the hard work Paul had been doing for him. "A man who does good work should be paid for it," then handed Paul an envelope full of what felt like cash. The fact that Paul said thank you and placed it in his pocket without counting it impressed Isaack.

"A man who gets an envelope full of cash and does not count it immediately... well, that shows good character, patience and trust. I like you Paul, you're calm all the time," Isaack stated, Paul smiled at Isaack.

"A man who impatiently counts money in front of the man that gifted it to him is rude, sir," Paul replied, and Isaack grinned at him.
"Like I said boy, I like you."

Paul spent the rest of the day on the firing range teaching some MLB members how to take a fixed position. He demonstrated this to them over and over and by the end of the day they still did not get it. Paul left the compound tired and frustrated. So, after Paul had driven home he decided to spend the rest of the night just hanging out at home alone with pizza, beer and maybe watch some Netflix.

Forty minutes later the pizza was delivered, and Paul used the cash Isaack gave him to pay for it, and it was then that Paul finally counted it.
"Shit, five thousand bucks, Isaack must like me," Paul said aloud to himself laughing. He sat down on his bed with his pizza, beer, and his tablet and started watching a movie about a superhero, allowing himself a rare moment to relax. Ten minutes later his cell phone rang once then stopped. This was the code that meant Reese was attempting contact. Paul walked over to the fridge, opened it, taking out the bar of butter and turned it over to retrieve the encrypted phone sealed in a Ziploc bag. He turned it on and sent a "???" in a text to Reese and waited while watching his movie.

Moments later the phone signaled he had received a text. "Come to my place now, please. Thomas is here to speak to you," the text said. Paul jumped up, replaced his phone in the butter and headed outside walking away from Reese's apartment like he was on an easy evening stroll. After about twenty minutes of zigzagging around the neighborhood he was sure he was not being followed and made his way to Reese's apartment.

Once Paul arrived at the apartment unseen he knocked on the door. Reese quickly pulled it opened, Paul entered, and she shut the door behind him. Thomas was there, and the two old friends gave each other the buddy hug, then Paul sat down at the kitchen table. Paul realized Reese's apartment was fully furnished. "Wait, you have a kitchen table and couch and shit?" Paul stated almost disbelieving.

"I basically only have a bed!" Paul added, directing his frustration towards Reese. "They told me I had to pay for everything myself and would be reimbursed later. Did you buy all this stuff?" She looked at him and shook her head.

"You were told to find an apartment, not rent the first apartment you seen on the Internet, stupid. I rented this one furnished. Try to use your brain for something other than hurting people!" Reese snapped at him.

Paul jumped up out of his chair looking at Reese. He was wanting to verbally attack her but could not find anything appropriate to say. Something about this woman strongly attracted him, even though he knew she never felt the same way towards him. Paul sat back down knowing he lost this round to her.

"What is it?" Paul asked, wanting to know what the meeting was all about. Thomas sat down with Reese, they wanted a full rundown on everything he had seen and heard over the past weeks and had about five hundred more questions needing answered. Paul told them everything that had happened and even handed over a few hundred bucks of the cash that Isaack had gave him, hoping they might be able to trace the money back somewhere. "Is that all the money he gave you?" Reese asked.

"Yep," Paul answered, then changed the topic telling them of the past few days, laughing as he told them about his altercation with Alfred and how that incident seemed to help him in the end. Reese explained that the FBI profile of Isaack shows that Isaack respects strength. The questions started again and went on and on for hours until Paul was getting frustrated and tired. "Christ, I have answered these same questions twice over and I need food! So, wrap this up. I got a double pepperoni at home that has gone way past cold," he said frustrated. "We are not done, and you can leave when we are," Reese said as she got up and went to the fridge. She retrieved some plastic bowls and warmed up some pasta she had made earlier that day and brought it to Paul along with a cold beer.

"Fuck yea!" Paul said aloud after his first bite, he took a drink of beer and began eating like he had not eaten for a week. Thomas looked at the beer and his lips felt dry and asked Reese if she had another for him. Reese ended up bringing one for him and one for herself. After a few minutes the mood in the room changed and before long they were laughing with each other having fun. Paul was on his fifth beer when he made the mistake of saying. "You know Reese, when you take the stick out of your ass, you are kind of fun." She looked at him and simply replied,

"Well Paul, when you stop acting like a dumb football jock turned shell shocked, depressed, veteran you are alright too." Paul and Reese looked at each other while Thomas laughed at both of them drinking another beer. Paul held up his beer and suggested,

"Truce." Reese smiled while nodding her head in approval.

Paul was tired and wanted to leave. "Well if we are done, I think I will leave," he said as he stood up.

"Sit down, we're not done," Thomas said, and Paul sat back down. "We need you to take a chance and do something to get in deeper, earn more of their trust or some shit," Thomas said. Paul looked at him confused.

"Please, tell me how I am supposed to fulfill this task Thomas?" Paul replied, holding his hands out to his sides. Thomas stood grabbing his notes and recorder, he then walked to the door and before leaving dropped,

"Paul, old buddy. You're a smart guy, figure it out." Then he walked out the door. Paul sat sitting at the kitchen table with Reese. "I have the strangest feeling of regret for saving his life in Iraq!"

Chapter 12.

June 01. Flint, Michigan.

 Paul was standing alone on the dark street in downtown Flint outside a club named Funk's. Timothy Jones had asked to meet him here for a beer this evening and talk about something that he said was important. Paul wondered why Jones had chose this particular place to talk. It was not a place he would have expected Jones to want to hangout in, plus the music was so loud he could hardly hear himself think, so he was standing outside listening to the band play. Paul looked again at the blue neon sign and was beginning to get very impatient waiting until he saw Jones pulling into a parking spot down the street. Paul began walking down the street towards Jones and yelled. "Hey, dip shit, you're late," as he was tapping his watch face.

 "Had to grab something," Jones replied with an odd grin on his face. The two met on the sidewalk, shook hands and went inside Funk's. They found a seat as far away from the band as possible, there was no surprise that the band was playing funk music.

 "I am surprised Jones, this place does not seem like your kind of hangout. I never figured you for funk music," Paul stated, and Jones laughed at him. "I hate this place," he shouted over the music as a young pretty black girl no more than twenty-two, walked up carrying a notepad and serving tray and asked for their drink orders. Both ordered a beer and the young girl smiled at them and hurried away. Moments later she returned with their drink order, Paul paid for both beers and gave the girl a nice tip of ten dollars. "What the hell are you tipping her for?" Jones asked in an angry sort of way.

"She brought the drinks fast and we never had to wait to order either. Besides, she is pretty and probably working her way through school, so why not?" Paul replied to Jones who did not respond, he just sat scanning the bar looking at everyone in the place like he was expecting to find someone. Paul could not help but notice Jones seemed nervous, maybe all jacked up angry about something. "Alright Jones, what is going on?" he asked him, leaning across the table. Jones took another drink of his beer as he continued scanning the club until he found what he was looking for.

"Midterms Paul," Jones said to him. Paul had no idea what he was talking about and most certainly Jones was not going to night school; Paul had doubts that the idiot could even spell midterm.

"What?" Paul asked. Jones just laughed again and pointed at a table with three black males in their early twenties who were sitting listening to the music, then said to Paul,

"Test night son. I want all three of those niggers sitting over there in the hospital, tonight!" Paul was silent for a minute, then asked Jones,

"Why?"

"To see if you can follow orders, and because I am ordering it!" Jones spat out quickly. Paul quickly finished his beer and thought to himself. "Well, Paul they told you to take a risk and gain their trust, so..." Paul stood up and walked over to the three black males minding their business as they watched the band on the stage. His stomach was moving into knots as his adrenaline began surging through his body making his heart rate speed up. As he walked closer to the young men he realized that the three young men were all wearing t-shirts from the University of Michigan. He was hoping they might have been some dead-beat gang bangers at least. He would enjoy hurting them, but college kids... "Shit," Paul said to himself. He walked up to the table looking at the boys trying to figure out what to say to make them want to fight, and the only thing that came to his mind was, "Get your black asses outside!" The three boys looked at each other in confusion.

"What the fuck, man?" the biggest one angrily said to Paul.

"Hey, I never said get to the back of the bus. I said move it outside! Didn't I blue gums." The largest one stood up visibly angry while Paul started walking to the doors as fast as he could, he did not want anything to happen inside. Paul moved out the door and headed down the street away from the windows of the club. He could hear them following him and getting closer, he stopped walking, then turned around just in time for the biggest one to take a running start and swing a hard-right hand at his face. Paul blocked it easily with his left forearm, then instantly countered with a straight right hand and struck the youngster in the throat, making him drop to the ground, both hands on his neck as he tried to breathe.

The second man also charged on Paul and tried to football tackle him, but Paul simple placed one hand on each of the boy's shoulders, stepped back and pushed down hard with his weight driving him face first into the concrete, sending him to sleep as some teeth rolled away.

The third came in smarter like a boxer, jabbing at Paul several times clearly looking to figure out some timing and the range. Paul waited for the boy to throw another punch and when he did, he lifted his right knee up and drove it deep into the young man's abdomen sending the boy to the ground holding his stomach gasping for air. Paul stood over all three and thought. "Wow, that was easy." Paul looked at all three making sure that they were all not in desperate need of medical assistance, then took a second quick look to the one he hit in the throat. The young man was beginning to stand when Paul kicked him in the ass sending him back down, then took off running down the street looking for Jones who was laughing at him and waving him over. Paul ran down the street to Jones who was climbing inside his black 2008 Ford Bronco. When Paul caught up to Jones he shouted while laughing for him to climb in the truck.

"Damn buddy you sure took care of them easy," Jones said while he laughed. Paul looked at him and held back the urge to crack his head open on the spot.

"They were just kids man," Paul said to him trying to hold back his disgust. Jones started the Bronco and sped away laughing. "Where are you taking me?" Paul asked him but then smelled a bad, familiar smell in the truck, "and why in the hell does it smell like gas in here?" Paul asked shouting then adding, "I suppose you want me to burn a cross for you or something?"

"The night is not over buddy. Midterm passed, but the final exam is yet to be held," Jones said even more excited than before.

"What is it?" Paul asked as he began to worry, but Jones said nothing and just continued to drive.

They drove outside of Flint to the north of the city a few miles into the darkness of the country. Jones turned off his headlights and drove a few miles in the dark before pulling off the road into a field and stopped the truck behind a large stack of hay bales.

"Okay buddy, this is it," Jones shouted excited. Paul looked at him and waited for some instructions. Jones giggled again while he climbed out of the Bronco and told Paul to follow him. Paul was getting worried, so before he opened his door he looked around to see if anyone else was in the area that might sneak up and shoot him, but it was clear as far as he could tell. Jones had climbed up the bale stack and sat down, Paul followed him up and sat down beside him.

"Okay Jones, what's up?" Paul asked him. Jones said nothing just pointed in the direction he was facing across the field through the darkness. Paul looked and made out what looked like an old country style church that had recently had some work done to it adding a large addition to it.

"See that old church?" Jones asked, and Paul nodded. "Good," Jones said and began explaining in the same cold manner. "Now in my Bronco there are two cans of gas. Now listen, one of those cans has a few sticks of dynamite taped to it. Go and burn that damn church to the ground." Paul was confused.

"You want me to go burn down a church?" Paul asked him disbelievingly and took another look at the old church with it's old style bell tower and thought the building must be over a hundred years old. Jones laughed again.

"It is not a real church. It is only for the darkies."

"Only for the darkies?" Paul asked aloud, disbelieving Jones was asking for this and realizing at that moment just how fucked the MLB must be. "Okay, but why?" Paul asked him.

"Because I said so! And Isaack said so! And if you don't do it someone else will. This is your final exam, son. Either do it or you are out! Besides, it is just a nigger church so who cares anyway." Paul climbed down from the bale stack thinking that every time Jones talks his voice made Paul want to have a small stroke. He went to Jones's Bronco and opened the back door. Inside he found the one box of wooden matches with two cans of gas, and one indeed had several sticks of dynamite taped to the side with a short fuse that might give Paul thirty seconds after it was lit.

Paul grabbed both cans and the matches and started walking the mile-long trek towards the church. "Yes buddy, I got front row seats," Jones said as he quietly cheered Paul onward. Paul walked silently towards the well-lit yard of the old church. It brought back the memory of a late-night raid on a Taliban compound in Afghanistan, except this mission made him feel like a real piece of shit.

Paul was wondering why they wanted this done and tried to remember why he was there in the first place. As he got closer, Paul changed his line of approach to allow him to access an area that was covered in trees which would take him to the new addition portion of the church on the backside which looked like a gymnasium. Once behind the gym he found a small gardening shed as well. Ten minutes later Paul had scouted the perimeter of the church and its grounds and was confident no one was in the building. He did notice before he broke the tree line a few security cameras, so he tore off a sleeve of his shirt and tied it around his face to avoid being identified later.

The first thing Paul did now was move to the shed on the backside of the gymnasium. It had a cheap lock securing the door which Paul broke off with one whack of a rock. He entered the shed finding a large amount of gardening tools as well as three barbeques, two lawnmowers, and another large can of gas. Paul removed all the propane tanks and took the other can of gas, then made his way to the gym door. Paul again ran the perimeter of the building checking all the doors looking for alarms, which from what he could tell, they all had.

He moved all the propane tanks to the back door of the gym and left the large can of gas there. He then ran the remaining cans to the to the front door and used an ice chipper he had removed from the garden shed to pry open the front door. As soon as the door opened an alarm sounded, Paul grabbed one can of gas leaving the one with the dynamite at the front door. He ran inside setting the gas can down on the floor in the middle of the room in the aisle between the pews, then ran down the isle towards the front when he saw a four-foot-tall carving of Christ on the cross hanging above the altar. Paul stopped and stared at Christ and Christ stared right back at him, at that moment Paul had the worst chills run down his spine he ever had. "I am definitely going to Hell now, no doubt about it," he said aloud. Getting back to business he ran into the new gymnasium portion of the church, opening the back door and bringing in the propane tanks and gas. Paul turned on all three of the propane tanks, then used the church's gas and poured it out all over the floor and bleachers all the way into the service section past

Jesus, who Paul was certain was still watching him. Once that can was empty he opened the other can pouring it around the alter and pews until the can was empty.

Paul ran to the front door, and took the third can with the dynamite taped to it, stood out to the door, pulled out the matches. He could hear police sirens coming from miles away and he knew he had to hurry. He lit the fuse and tossed the can as deep inside the church. He began running into the field and the safety of the darkness as fast as he could go heading back to Jones. Paul counted the seconds to himself as he ran. He had guessed it was a thirty second fuzz but when it went off Paul was only at twenty-six seconds and the church was engulfed in flames almost instantly. "What have I done?" Paul asked himself aloud, almost breaking down into tears as he continued to run.

Paul sprinted back to the bale stack where Jones was waiting cheering him along. When Paul got to the Bronco, Jones was sitting in it with the motor running, and they drove off heading deeper into the countryside away from the oncoming police. Paul sat quietly catching his breath while Jones welcomed him to the MLB, calling him brother and going on and on about the new country they were going to build after they destroyed the old one. Paul sat silently listening to Jones jabber on as they took the long way home back into town to Paul's truck.

"Why did we do this Jones?" Paul asked.

"To stir up the population, racial tensions man," Jones said proudly.

"You think one church will stir things up?" Paul asked him.

"Buddy just watch the news in the morning," Jones giggled and pulled into the parking spot directly behind Paul's truck. Jones's phone beeped, and he pulled it from his jacket pocket and read the text on the screen. "Isaack says welcome to the MLB." Jones said to him as he exited the Bronco, Paul just nodded. "He says for you to come to the compound for lunch tomorrow, we have more to talk about," Jones said to him and Paul simply gave him a thumb up in return and shut the door.

He walked over to his truck and drove to his apartment while thinking the entire way of the horrible thing he had done tonight. Paul had killed many times in his military career and he was always content with his actions in battle. But tonight, Paul was sick to his stomach after beating those three college kids and burning the church and he felt ashamed. He thought about his dad knowing that deep inside part of the reason he was doing this was for some atonement for the disappointment he had been to his father, and after tonight he knew he felt he had let him down again.

He pulled up to his apartment and instead of going inside he found himself walking down the street to Reese's. It was late, but he did not care and knocked on the door, a moment later she opened her door and was wearing a Coke-a-cola t-shirt and pajama bottoms. She was holding her FBI issue Sig Sauer P-226 in her hand and was still half asleep. She woke up fast when she saw the look on Paul's face and instantly drug him inside.

"Did anyone see you come here?" she asked him.

"No, trust me no one is watching me anymore," Paul said emotionless.

"What happened? Did you hurt someone?" she asked, her curiosity spiked greatly.

"I am one of them now," Paul said almost breaking into tears then added, "They trust me as a brother now." Reese looked at him and became very worried. She took his hand and held it tight.

"Paul look at me, what did you do?" He began telling her the story of the night's events and she listened carefully taking in all the details. "Animals!" Reese said in disgust of what they had asked Paul to do. He stood up, "I am sorry Reese, I should not have woken you. I need to go to bed." Paul said to her as he made his way to the door. She followed him to the door and before he took the doorknob she, wrapped both arms around his neck and gave him a hug and held him in tight. Paul wrapped his hands around her waist and pulled her tight into his body. She smelled so good to him, and he began getting aroused and pulled away. She looked at him and took his hand again and pulled him to her and kissed him on the neck. Paul lowered his head and she kissed him hard on the mouth and asked,

"Do you want to stay?" He looked at her and quietly whispered,

"Yes." Reese smiled then lead him down the hall not to the bedroom but to the bathroom.

"Then you must shower before you get into my bed, because you stink of gasoline."

Chapter 13.

June 2.nd,Flint, Michigan.

   Paul woke the next morning still at Reese's apartment, the smell of bacon and coffee tickled his nostrils like someone throwing a bucket of cold water on him. He rolled out of bed stretching his arms out and letting out a silent yawn before dressing himself, then leaving the bedroom following his nose for the coffee. "Morning, is the coffee free?" Paul joked then gently poked Reese in the ribs, she smiled at him as she reached for the cupboard to retrieve a cup. She was wearing a dark blue bath robe and Paul took advantage of it by taking hold of the belt and pulled her into him kissing her neck. Even after last night's hours of coitus he wanted her even more this morning as he spun her around and tried to undo the front. She pushed him away laughing.

   "I am hungry, not right now!" she said smiling as she reached down and pinched his groin, then poured him a coffee. Paul took the hot black coffee into the living room and sat down turning on the TV and channel searched for the local morning news. Jones had said check the news in the morning and once he found the channel he was looking for he set the remote down waiting for the commercials to stop and the news to start.
Paul was happy this morning, happier than he had been in a long time, maybe it was because he just had sex four, or was it five times with one of the prettiest girls he had ever seen. He felt different

this morning and it only took him a second to figure it out, she had given him back some much needed confidence, and he was liking it, he was hoping the feeling would stick around.

He returned his attention back to the TV when the commercials stopped, and the headline news started, Paul was expecting maybe to see something on the fire he set last night, but what he saw surprised and shocked him more than he could imagine. Around the nation over fifty churches, mosques and two Jewish temples had been burned to the ground or vandalized. Almost every church that had been hit catered to black, Hispanic or gay people. There was uproar all over the nation and people of color were already marching everywhere in protest. "This is why Jones told me to watch the news this morning," Paul said sadly as Reese stood behind him staring at the TV.

"These people are fucking crazy," Reese said, shocked and returned to the kitchen.

"I am going to bring them down," Paul said aloud and turned off the TV and walked into the kitchen and sat with Reese. They tried to enjoy their breakfast, but both said little to each other. Reese could see Paul was angry as he shoved food into his mouth like he had not eaten in weeks. She finally broke the silence.

"Paul, when do you go to see Isaack?" she asked concerned.

"In a couple of hours," Paul answered taking a big bite of toast. She set her fork down, stood up and walked over to him sitting in the chair next to his.

"What about us?" she asked him. Paul got nervous, he was really hoping this might carry on with her, he really liked her and well, her eggs were amazing too. Paul took a drink of coffee before answering her, then he looked at her and gripped her hand.

"Well, I guess that is up to you. I was kind of hoping we may spend more time together," he said softly. Reese let out a big sigh and kissed Paul and returned to her meal.

A few hours later Paul walked through the gate house at the MLB compound unchecked this day. He had proven himself loyal and the color on his gate pass was now green allowing access to all areas in the compound. Paul had shown up as directed for a lunch at Isaack's house and was picked up by Jones at the gate. "You seem happy this morning." Jones said, Paul put on a fake smile and said,

"Turned on the news this morning like you said and guess what I saw?" Jones laughed out loud and yelled.

"Won't be long now!" Then he sped up the Gator as they headed for Isaack's house.

They pulled up to Isaack's house and walked up to the guards who directed them to go out back like last time, except Paul was not disarmed or searched this time and was allowed to move unescorted.

"Paul, Jones," Isaack shouted as he stood and gave both men a hug. He had been sitting outside watching CNN all morning grinning and smoking cigarettes, while bathing in his success. "Sit down and watch the news with me. Some white families got hurt as they drove by a burning church in Kentucky last night. Tensions are rising in this country. Damn shame!" Isaack said while shaking his head. The three sat down and Isaack's wife brought them some coffee and told them lunch would be served soon, then returned to the kitchen. "You did good last night Paul," Isaack said.

"Well, I wish I would have known what was up. I could have dressed for the occasion," Paul said back. Isaack was looking at Paul in the eyes again and smiled,

"You have changed," Isaack said, and Paul was unsure what he was insinuating. "You got a taste for it last night and have changed," Isaack repeated.

"Sir?" Paul stated confused.

"When a warrior finds his true calling he accepts the beast inside him. The beast then settles down and stops torturing the warrior's soul, and the warrior is able to rest because it has found its true place and settled down," Isaack explained, "and you Paul Totten are rested this day." Paul sat listening to Isaack and again thought, how well this man can speak.

They finished their soup and sandwiches, then Isaack got down to business. "I have a mission for both of you," Isaack said, sounding like the general he claimed to be. "I need you to go to Elk Heart, Indiana," Isaack explained. Paul sat listening intently, Jones was excited and Paul guessed he was hoping to hurt some people. Jones, you remember old Reggie Bolton, don't you?" Jones nodded.

"Yea, the old nut who lives alone in that old shack with all the guns." Isaack smiled and began explaining.

"Good, I have maps and money, everything you will need waiting for you at the gate house now listen up, you will be leaving immediately. Drive to Elkhart and discretely move into the woods near Reggie's place. Do not, I stress, do NOT let anyone see you. When you get close phone both the ATF and the local police station on the phones in the bag at the gatehouse, the numbers are in there for you, and tell them Reggie is shooting at you. They will believe this, because he is a well-known gun freak and certifiably paranoid. Once the first police car comes, shoot it up using the rifle at the gate house. I don't care if you kill the cops or not, but you will stop the police on the road. Then leave, destroy the phone, dispose of the rifle and do not get caught," Isaack explained, and Paul understood what he had to do it was an easy plan, but he could not figure why.

Paul waited for Isaack to stop talking before he asked,

"Sir, I get the plan, but can you inform us as to why we are setting up an old man?" Isaack smiled and thought for a second, then decided he would let them both in.

"Okay, Reggie is a known loner and nut. He collects guns but only legal stuff and is incredibly paranoid. So, when the cops come to his house in force after we stir them up and shoot up the cruiser. Reggie will go ballistic and probably open fire." Isaack explained, but Paul was still not getting it and shook his head at Isaack. "He only has legal guns, so if they kill him all the gun crazy guys, and the second amendment right activists will start protesting."
Paul finally understood, and he wanted to kill Isaack sitting there smoking that stinking cigarette. "Stirring up the population!" Isaack said proudly. Setting up a loner who just wants to be left to his own life is bullshit, Paul thought and the rage inside him was burning in his stomach. "Well, get going!" Isaack ordered.

They drove back to the gate house to find Alfred waiting for him with their mission package. It contained an old Winchester 3030 lever action deer rifle, an envelope with two thousand dollars, the keys to an older model Dodge Dakota and three cell phones.

"Hey, Alfred," Paul said trying to greet Alfred hoping they could bury the hatchet.

"Fuck you Paul!" he said back with his bruised face turning red. Paul snickered as he really did not care. "Give me your phones and wallets!" Alfred ordered, Paul looked at him like he was crazy. "You know the rules, nothing to lead them back here and remember if you're caught say nothing." Alfred snapped in a threatening manner.

"Okay man, relax," Paul said and handed over his things.

The drive to Elkhart took them almost three hours and it was now almost five o'clock.

"So, you know this guy?" Paul asked Jones.

"Yea I have met him a few times. He is like Isaack said, a real screwball who goes nuts and scares everyone around the area with his threats and shit. He has come to a few rallies over the years and just caused trouble when he gets drunk. I have bought a few really good deer rifles off him and trust me that is the only good thing about this man."
Paul said nothing back. He was deep in thought trying to figure out a way to save this man's life without breaking his cover. He thought of maybe just killing Jones, but then people would ask questions.

Paul opened the envelope that was provided to them and looked at the notes provided. He read the instructions, and they would be put up in a hotel on the outside of Elkhart that someone else had rented for them, the keys would be given to them in the parking lot. Jones wanted to recon the area the night before hand, so they continued to the country road close to Reggie's place.

Thirty minutes later they pulled off the road and walked into the woods two miles from Reggie's shack. Paul and Jones made their way through the bush as silently as possible, but Jones seemed to find and step on every branch that had ever fell off a tree in Indiana.

"Christ Jones, be quiet or go back to the truck!" Paul whispered and started walking again. The darkness was coming in fast and in the bushes, it made it even darker. It took about ten more feet when Jones stepped on another twig causing a loud snap. Paul lost his cool and grabbed Jones by the shirt pulling him close. "Go back to the truck and wait for me or I swear to god Jones I will crack your fucking head!" Paul said it as if it was a promise. Jones said nothing. He just walked back towards the truck. Paul thought he may have scared Jones some, but really Paul didn't care, the man was an idiot.

Paul crept up on the shack it had been a lot farther into the woods than he thought. There in a clearing was a small fenced off compound with several small sheds that were built side by side, all had three solar panels on the roofs. A large fire pit was in the middle of the compound and roared loud with flames eight feet high. An older fat man danced around the fire laughing alone with a bottle of bourbon in his hand more than half gone.

Paul watched as Reggie fell on his butt on the ground laughing and singing, and had a hard time getting back up to his feet. Paul could see two more bottles sitting out on a metal barrel still full. "The old bastard is having a party." Paul thought to himself and had an idea. Paul realized, if he could get the police to come out here tonight, the way Reggie was pounding the bourbon he would be asleep when they got here, therefore no gunfight.

Paul silently made his way back to the truck and Jones was sitting in the driver's seat and as soon as Paul opened the door he said to Paul,

"Sorry bro." Paul laughed and accepted his apology, then told him they were doing it tonight.

"What the hell do you mean tonight?" Jones asked.

"Yea, I seen him packing a bag. I think he is going hunting or something tomorrow so let's do it tonight before he leaves." Paul made that line of bullshit up on the spot as he said it and thought what a damn good liar he was becoming.

The two sat planning how to do it while Paul loaded the rifle after wiping each round down making sure all prints were off the brass in case he lost any in the night. They drove back down to the main road where both men took a phone. Paul jumped out and ran into the trees with the rifle while Jones headed down the road to the designated pickup spot two miles away. Paul sat down in the trees with the rifle and waited for someone to drive past. It didn't take long, and it was only a few minutes before Paul could see headlights coming. As the vehicle got closer Paul noticed it was a larger truck pulling a horse trailer behind it. He decided to let it pass as he was afraid the operator may lose control pulling the trailer when he got the fright of his life and crash with the heavy load behind him.

A few minutes later another vehicle came along and this time he noticed it was a normal sized pickup truck and he could see the occupant was alone as it got closer. Paul raised the old Winchester and looked down the iron sites aiming for the headlight and fired. The driver's side headlight shattered, and the driver went into shock as he jerked on the steering wheel while slamming on the brakes coming to a stop. Paul suspected the driver did not know what happened, so when the confused man got out of the truck, Paul fired another round into the windshield and howled like a wolf in the air and fired into the air again, making sure he collected the brass after each time he fired. The man jumped back in the truck and sped away fast.

Paul reloaded the rifle and then leaned it against a tree pulling out the cell phone and opened the flip door calling 911. After he gave a panic sounding call to the operator he hung up the phone and turned it off, placing it into his pocket and picked up the rifle. They were only twenty miles from town, Paul figured it would not take long for some unlucky cop to show up out here this night, and he was right. Less than ten minutes later he could see police lights coming down the road and he could hear the cruiser speeding on the gravel road from a long way off. The officer did not have a siren blaring and slowed down almost to a crawl as he approached the turnoff to Reggie's compound. Paul lifted the rifle to his shoulder took careful aim and shot out the right front tire, then he shot out the left front tire. He then quickly moved positions running father away. The cruiser stopped almost immediately, and a county sheriff jumped out hiding behind the car.

"God, damn it Reggie! It is Norman, hold your goddamn fire!" the sheriff shouted. Paul fired again knocking off one of the lights from the roof of the car. Paul could hear the deputy on the radio calling for backup, Paul then fired again, taking out another light on the top of the cruiser. Paul quietly slipped deeper into the woods keeping out of sight, then headed towards Jones.

The night was dark and after five hundred yards in the woods Paul went back to the road and began running flat out to gain more distance. Paul was satisfied how everything had gone and he guessed Reggie would be passed out cold about now, and the cops would be sending everyone they had after him and there should be no problems Paul thought. As Paul ran over a small bridge that crossed a stream, he left the road and climbed down to the mud. He took the rifle barrel pointing down and pressed it down into the mud.

Once it was down in the mud there was only the stock showing, he put his foot on the stock and stood on it making it slide deeper into the mud completely submerging it. Then to make it better he took a handful of mud and covered his footprint and used some water to smooth it over. He then washed his hands and took off running again towards Jones.

Once he made it to the appointed spot Jones was standing on the road waiting for Paul. "I heard the shooting," Jones whispered. Paul was exhausted after running the two miles and he thought Jones would be at what turned out to be three and he did it all at a run. "Well, did you kill that cop?" Jones asked him excited.

"No, I wanted him to call it in. Did you call the ATF?" Paul asked trying to catch his breath.

"Yep, all good." Jones said grinning ear to ear. Paul jumped in the truck and told Jones to get in and drive. They headed straight back to Flint not spending the night in Elkhart and only stopping in Battle Creek for some food, then they finished the drive home, trashing the cell phones and tossing them out the window after crossing the state line.

After returning to the compound he retrieved his wallet and phone, it was close to five am, Paul was exhausted. He drove back to his apartment and climbed into his bed. He picked up his tablet and checked the news feeds from Elkhart and found a headline he was wishing he had not. "CRAZIED GUNMAN KILLS SHERRIF'S DEPUTY IN ARMED

STAND OFF." Paul sat the tablet on the bedside table saying aloud. "What did I do?"

Chapter 14.

June 17. Flint, Michigan.

Paul never told Reese right away about the trip to Elkhart, not because he was afraid to, but he was unable to. She had been called away to Washington leaving a message for Paul on the encrypted phone for him. The day after he had returned from Elkhart, Paul watched the news regularly looking for details on the events from the night before. The details he had read the night before when he had first returned were inaccurate. No police officers had been killed but, one had been wounded and shot in the leg by Reggie as he approached the compound, officers had returned fire immediately killing him.

In the coming days information had came in that Reggie had nothing illegal on the compound and the weapon that discharged at the police was never recovered from his compound. Even the land beside the road that the shooter had been hiding in did not belong to Reggie.

Isaack was right, the second amendment activists crawled all over the police and were protesting the actions the police took after the event on the road and were claiming they had jumped to conclusions and tensions rose higher across the nation.

There had even been a clash between gun rights activists and a Black Lives Matter group after a police shooting in Baltimore. While in two other cities peaceful demonstrations resulted in the crowd being teargassed before trouble had began.

Witnesses in both cities claimed they saw a white uniformed police officer throw the gas grenade into the peaceful crowds. The police claimed they were not responsible, and even proved by inventory of the serial numbers that their complete arsenal was still present, and the gas grenades recovered from both scenes did not come from their arsenals. But it did not matter, tensions rose even higher. Paul knew this was Isaack's masterminding to stir up the population with hatred and distrust.

Paul had decided not to go to the compound this day, he just sat in his apartment relaxing and basically doing nothing. He had finally bought a couch and coffee table but still no kitchen table. For the past week, he had been teaching some of the MLB members how to live in the woods for a prolonged period of time unseen and staying healthy. So today was his and he was hoping he could see Reese somehow this night, he had much to tell her and he wanted to spend time with her, but most importantly he wanted out of the MLB assignment. "Surely, they have enough on Isaack to shut him down by now," he thought.

A few hours later he received one ring on his phone then it stopped, he checked the encrypted phone and a message to "come see me" was waiting for him. Paul changed clothes and went outside on his walk for a few blocks, until he confirmed no one was following and then he redirected himself to Reese's apartment.

She opened the door pulling him inside and closing it quickly behind him and began pulling off his clothes.

"Business second, I have missed you," she said as she lifted his shirt over his head. Paul was surprised by her aggressiveness but was happy, he was hoping for the same thing.

After the session of intimacy was finished they sat naked on the bed talking. Paul had told her everything that had happened over the past twelve days, from Elkhart to the woodland training session he had completed. Reese was shocked when he told her of Elkhart, then left the bedroom. She returned a moment later with some paper and pen and began taking notes and began asking questions. Paul now asked her if they had enough to arrest Isaack and shut down the MLB. "I am sorry Paul, we need info on the weapons and who in the government is helping them," she explained disappointing him. Paul just sat there laying in bed gently running his fingers over her soft skin on her back.

Reese set the notepad down on the table next to the bed and placed her head on Paul's chest. "What are you going to do after this is over?" she asked him. He looked at her and started thinking as he had not really thought about it.

"I have not thought about it to be truthful. Since my release from the army it has been one thing after another. Maybe CIG will hire me, or maybe I will end up waiting tables, or a carney cleaning up some elephant shit," he said smiling.

"Come on Paul, I know your dad left you some money and you have been given a pension. You don't need to wait tables. You can wait and find a good job someplace," Reese said wanting him to be serious. Paul rolled her over on her back and looked into her eyes.

"Honestly Reese, I don't know. By the look on your face I think you have something in mind for me." Her face turned red somewhat and she nervously said,

"I was hoping you would come with me and maybe stay at my place in Washington." Paul listened to her and smiled.

"I think that would be nice," he said.

Chapter 15.

June 18. Washington D.C. L'Efant Plaza Hotel.

Martin Sibley and Allen Costner entered the L'Enfant Plaza Hotel and went directly to the elevator and pressed the button for up and waited. Once the door opened they entered and quickly pressed the button for the third floor. "I can't believe this idiot wants to see me in person. I would think he would understand the risks of us being seen talking to each other." Martin said with an angry tone.

Martin and Costner had left Martin's house unseen by driving Costner's car that he had parked inside the garage. Martin had laid down in the back seat and Costner drove away while the Secret Service smiled and waved goodbye at him. The ball cap and sunglasses Martin wore this night did an excellent job at hiding his identity and no one had noticed him as he walked through the lobby.

They left the elevator and walked down the recently renovated hallway to room three-twenty-one. Costner knocked on the door and it was Isaack Elzey who opened it letting them inside, then closed and locked the door behind them. Isaack collected all the phones and placed them into the bathroom and closed that door as well. Martin took a good look around the room at the new furnishings and clean carpets. "Nice," he thought he would have to bring his mistress here one night.

"Okay boys." Isaack said as he lit a cigarette. "We will be getting to this right away, just one more minute," he added while Martin glared at him.

"I can not believe how stupid you are! Demanding to meet me like this! What would happen if you were being followed?" Martin snapped at Isaack.

"Relax, Martin old friend. I was not followed, we took every precaution."

"We!" Martin snapped, as a sudden knock on the door made Martin jump. Isaack smiled at Martin and walked to the door and pulled it open allowing Boris to walk in. Martin began to lose control as he saw the Russian walk into the room. "Do you have any idea what a risk this is?" Martin yelled. Boris walked up to Martin and reached over and grabbed his hand shaking it hard and said in his deep Russian accent.

"My friend, it is good to see you." Then he walked across the room and opened the mini bar and retrieved a beer then sat down at the desk. "I will say this once Martin. Do not yell at me again! You have not forgotten our arrangement, have you?" Boris alluded like he was stating a threat when in fact he was. Martin quieted down and said,

"No, I have not forgotten our arrangement." Boris smiled arrogantly at Martin.

"Good, let's get to it," Boris said and pointed to Isaack who walked to the center of the room and began speaking. "We have moved our timetable ahead by three months. I have almost recruited enough people. Anymore in mind could be reckless and might result in law enforcement gaining access to the organization. Very few people know of our plans and the rank and file will not know until we are about to pull off the act," Isaack explained. Boris raised his hand. "Will you have enough weapons in three months?" he asked. "We have more than enough for the act now. The next shipments that we will be receiving from now until the revolution will be spread about for the war after the White House has been burned to the ground. Martin held his hand up now.

"I want Sterling Hunton killed!" he blurted.

"Make sure you know his location on the day and we will kill him," Isaack calmly replied.

"So, it is coming then? The revolution is coming and is only months away. I never thought I would see the day," Martin stated like he was in a fantasy. Boris stood and walked over to Martin.

"Remember after you are placed in power, Eastern Europe is ours! We will make sure you are in power and in return, the file I have on you will remain hidden. Unless you interfere in Russia's affairs," Boris stated sternly. Martin was smiling like a kid waiting to enter the front gates of Disneyland. Isaack stood listening while he lit another cigarette.

"As far we are concerned Russia can have all of Europe. After we take power, America will isolate itself from the world to straighten itself out and let the world sort itself out," Isaack explained.

"Isaack, I will have the rest of the money delivered to you soon, and I will speed up the weapons deliveries as well," Boris explained. Costner stepped forward wanting to speak.

"Isaack, are the accommodations complete for the VIPs to wait out the war in safety and the accommodations for the less than co-operative?" Isaack laughed.

"What is wrong Costner? Are you not planning to get your hands dirty in the fighting? I have six bunkers built in six states each big enough for twelve people. Also, I have a prison built in an old dairy barn with enough cells for two hundred people. Everything is to the plan and everything is ahead of schedule," Isaack explained, and everyone seemed content with the plan.

"So, this is it then?" Costner asked. "We will not be meeting again in person until the revolution has begun," Costner added. Martin went to the minibar, opening it and grabbing enough small bottles of vodka and whiskey for everyone and then handed them out. He opened his and held it high.

"Gentlemen a toast please, to a new America and a new Russia." Martin was grinning,

"Please Boris pass on to President Shuisky that when I am in power I hope our two nations can work together in friendship." Boris smiled at

Martin and held his bottle up acknowledging Martin's request.

Chapter 16.

July 1. Flint, Michigan.

It was approaching noon this day as Paul followed the directions given to him by Jones to a small farm about forty miles south of Flint. He pulled into the lane way slowing down and took a good look at the yard seeing a high flying American flag upside down on a pole in front of the old house. He remembered reading someplace that an upside-down flag was a sign of distress in the US military.

"Idiots and freaks." Paul said aloud to himself. This house had to have been the oldest house still standing in Michigan. It was constructed from logs, looked like only it had about three rooms, and the occupants still used an old outhouse located forty feet from the front step.

A man in his thirties walked out of the front door, Paul had seen around the MLB compound a few times, but had never had the pleasure of knowing his name. The unknown man waved Paul to drive behind the house to a barn that had to be older than the house, and as he rounded the house he saw Jones' SUV parked beside another old Dodge pickup.

As Paul pulled up to the barn, Jones stepped out waving to Paul like they were old friends. Paul shut his truck off and stepped out, "Paul, buddy what the hell took you so long? Leave your phone and wallet in the truck and get in here, we got work to do this night." Paul left his things in his pick up and followed him inside the old barn. When he walked in he saw the things he had been sent inside the MLB for all those long weeks ago, weapons. Paul had found the weapons, well some anyway. Paul began walking around doing a fast count, trying to keep an inventory in his mind. He found at least ten RPG-7s and could see over thirty rockets for reloading and dozens of rifles along with crates of ammunition. There was various types of explosives and different equipment. "Shit Paul, get over here would you," Jones shouted while grinning at him, knowing he was blown away with what he saw. "This is a small stash man, some of our stashes are five times this big," Jones said calmly as he loaded bullets inside a pistol magazine. Paul looked at the two men with Jones, he had seen them around and knew them both, twin brothers Eric and Lee Vos. Both were farm boys from outside of Flint and both were ex-army. They came back from Iraq messed up like so many others and found Isaack made them feel like they belonged again. Paul watched them loading mags while talking to each other. They were both six feet tall, slim, but not skinny, and not physically fit. Both had blonde hair and dressed like farm boys in checkered shirts. Doug wore blue and Eric wore red, or was it the other way around? Paul had a hard time telling sometimes.

Paul walked over to the table and greeted the brothers while Jones handed him a pistol. A Makarov 9x18 .380 and two mags then said, "Well

shit Paul, I am not loading your weapon for you."
Paul grabbed a pair of rubber latex gloves then
donned them like the others so not to leave any
prints on any casings they might leave behind. He
picked up a mag and reached into the ammo box
and began pressing the bullets into his mags. Paul
had no idea what was going on, but guessed they
were going to kill someone. After the incident with
Reggie, Paul promised himself that no more
innocent people would die if he could help it, and if
that meant killing Jones and these other two idiots,
well then so be it.

Paul waited about a minute to ask Jones,

"Alright Jones what is going on? What do we
need the weapons for?" Paul asked impatiently.

"We are going to Chicago, to meet some bad ass
Mexicans and pick up a little bit of cash."

"Chicago?" Paul asked disbelievingly.

"Yes, Chicago and we are taking guns because you
never trust a Mexican cartel thug."

"Cartel...Cartel. Holy shit Jones, if were doing
business with the Cartel I want more than an eight
shot Makarov." Paul said with a raised voice, he
then walked over taking an older AK-47 that was
leaning against the wall then walked over to
another crate, picked up a couple mags and found
the ammo for them, and began loading them.
Jones was laughing at Paul again and then looked
over at the twins and said,

"See, told you he would be in."

The four drove to Chicago in an older white Chevy Suburban. Paul placed the rifle in the back under a blanket and kept the pistol in the front pocket of his hoodie with the extra mag in his front left pants pocket. The drive took almost six hours to get to Chicago and another thirty minutes to find the place they were going to. They ended up in the lower west side in what looked like a particularly bad part of town. Gang graffiti covered many walls and young men stood on corners with many wearing bandanas showing their gang colors on various parts of their bodies.

Paul was sitting in the back seat on the passenger side while Jones drove, the two brothers told stories of their tours in Iraq almost the entire way, which made the trip almost enjoyable. "Okay, we are there," Jones announced oddly calm for a cartel deal. Jones turned into a large fenced area filled with warehouses, then pulled over and stopped. He picked up a cell phone, dialed a number and had a brief conversation with someone named Havier, telling him they were there and then hung up. Jones then started driving again, then slowly turned to the left pulled up to a large overhead door and honked the horn three times. There were numerous older cars of various makes that were parked out front had been or were in the process of being fixed up. The overhead door opened, Jones waited a moment for the door to raise then slowly drove into the large body shop and vehicle restoration company.

There were at least a dozen cars parked inside being worked on, counters full of tools and equipment everywhere.

As soon as they entered the building the door shut behind them and eight Latino looking men calmly walked out surrounding the Suburban. Paul looked around counting them and taking notice that they were all armed.

"Shit!" Paul said aloud.

"It is okay, stay in the truck," Jones said as he slowly exited the vehicle and walked over to converse with the only one that was not dressed like a complete thug. Paul continued looking around the Suburban at the men surrounding them. They all appeared angry, Paul could see it on their faces, or maybe that was an act to intimidate them. They all were covered in tattoos and from head to toe, some had bandanas, but all wore baggy jeans and white tank tops. Paul reached into the back when Jones began talking and quickly pulled the rifle over the seat into his lap. Jones was talking to the man who Paul assumed was the boss he had called Havier on the phone. The boss called for one of his men in Spanish to go and get something. The young Mexican did what he was told running away to an office, then came back quickly with three large duffel bags. There was one on his shoulder and one in each hand and he dropped them in front of Jones' feet. He picked them up and brought them to the Suburban, opened the back gate, tossing them in and piled them up. Then without saying another word he walked around and climbed in, quickly started the vehicle. One of the men opened the door and Jones quickly backed out of the shop.

"Well, that was easy," Paul stated, then Jones laughed out loud.

"Of course, fifty million dollars in those bags boys, fifty million bones."

"Holy shit!" Paul stated in surprise and turned around in his seat unzipping one bag to see what fifty million bucks looked like and was blown away by the sight of all that cash. "Wow," Paul shouted excitedly, and one of the brothers gave a loud "Whoop." The four were excited to get away from the cartel alive and immediately started the long drive home. Paul took another look in the back to see the bags again, but before he turned front again he noticed an older beat up Cadillac behind them with two black males. He paid them little mind and turned front again. Jones drove the speed limit and the four laughed and teased each other about how scared they were in the garage. After several blocks, Paul casually looked behind them again and noticed the same caddy was still behind them.

"Shit, I think were being followed," Paul stated nervously, the other three men all turned and looked behind them and became instantly nervous. "Just relax," Paul told them, then he told Jones, "Keep driving, try and get to a more public area." Jones picked up the phone and called Havier explaining they were being followed and asked if it was him.

"No, they are black," Jones explained to Havier and a minute later he hung up the phone. "It is not Havier's people, he said they have been having some shipments jacked by a black crew, he thinks these guys are them," Jones explained. "Havier said to try get and get back to him for help," Jones said as he took a right turn drove a block and made another turn. Paul looked behind them again and noticed two vehicles were following with three more black males. Another car sped up behind them with two more men inside. Paul watched as the man in the passenger seat pulled out a cell phone and put it to his ear. Paul reached down grabbing the AK laying it on the bags with the muzzle pointed behind them and kept his seated position facing backwards watching them closely. Jones said,

"Five blocks and we are back at the warehouse." Then he slammed on the brakes propelling Paul backwards into the front seat as the Suburban skidded to a stop.

Paul righted himself in the seat again looking back at the three cars behind them with the seven men in them, then quickly looked to the front to see why Jones had stopped so suddenly. There were two cars blocking the road with four men pointing guns at them. Paul saw the three cars behind them stop and the seven-armed men riding in them stepped out. Paul took another look at both sides and saw an alleyway to the left.

"Jones, see the alley to the left? Go for it when I open up. Twins, shoot the guys up front." All three men acknowledged Paul's orders. Paul picked up the rifle and put it to his shoulder waiting for the moment. The men on both sides screamed at them to exit the vehicle, one of the hijackers to the front took a shotgun and fired a round into the windshield, while one in the back fired a burst from a Tech nine into the lower part of the back door, with one round hitting Eric in the lower back, or was it Lee. Paul tightened on the rifle and yelled. "Cover your ears!"

Then he began burst firing out the back of the Suburban making the back window explode like he was laying down hellfire. "Jones, move!" Paul yelled then, letting go anther burst at the men behind them as they were diving for cover. Paul noticed he had hit two of them as Jones turned the Suburban heading towards the alley. The hijackers opened fire hitting the truck on multiple spots but thankfully none hit flesh, but the wounded twin was screaming in pain. The other rolled his window down and returned fire as Jones crossed the street and sped into the alley away from the hijackers. Paul kept looking back making sure and hoping they were not being followed, but as his luck would have it the caddy turned into the alley with four men in it speeding towards them.

Jones yelled that they had lost a tire on the front and the steering was pulling to the right and driving was becoming harder. Paul let another burst go at the caddy hoping they might slow down, but it had little effect as the gangsters closed the distance with them.

They exited the alley back onto a street and Jones was turning left again trying to get Havier on the phone again. Trying to make the left turn at high speed with a flat front tire was too hard for Jones while he was trying to dial the phone, and he crashed them into a parked car.

People on the street ran for their lives when they saw Paul quickly changing the mag in the rifle as he climbed over the bags of money and out the back window. He ran to the entrance of the alley and waited for the hijacker's caddy to come speeding towards them. Paul lifted the rifle and squeezed the trigger, he fired the entire magazine in short bursts into the oncoming car. After the first ten rounds the car lost control after the driver was hit and crashed into the wall of the building and it stopped him dead. Paul finished off the other three men with the remaining rounds as they were scrambling to get out of the car.

Jones had got the suburban moving again and called for Paul, who was already climbing through the back window screaming for him to move. They made the drive back to the body shop with a flat tire, steaming radiator and no more problems. The cartel thugs opened the door for them, allowing them to drive right in. Some members left the garage to go looking for more of the hijackers. One of the young men opened the door and helped the wounded twin out, while another ran for a first aid kit. Havier walked up looking at the wounded twin and stated in his heavy accent,

"Bad business those Black Warriors. They are a hit crew who hijack other crew's loads. They were most likely watching us and thought you had a load of blow, you know? They are hard to find and there is only about ten of them." Paul walked around the Suburban and said,

"No. there is only about four, I got six." Havier laughed out loud,

"Good work man," he shouted smiling, "We have... well, kind of a doctor, I will call him for your friend. Then we will hook you up with a new ride for your drive home and escort you out of town. Okay bro? I feel bad for the mishap, I wouldn't want to piss you guys off by losing Grimes' money. My boss would literally kill me." Grimes. Paul heard him say the name Grimes and Grimes was mixed up somehow with the Mexican cartel, sending money to Isaack. Paul knew he would have to remember that name.

Chapter 17.

July 10. Flint, Michigan.

It had taken Paul, Jones and the twins almost ten days to get out of Chicago and back to Flint, the police were searching hard for four white males driving a white Suburban who had killed six black males, which believe it or not helped in increasing the racial tensions around Chicago. Paul, Jones and the brothers stayed in that damn dirty body shop for nine days, until the heat had died down and the wounded Vos brother was well enough to move. The cartel guys were cool though, they brought in mattresses, food and kept them entertained for the time they sat there with nothing to do. Paul even took the time and learned a little about auto body work and made plans to paint his dad's old truck when he was done with this undercover work.

They had arrived home in the morning, Isaack was delighted even after they were ten days late getting home. Jones praised Paul to Isaack telling him it was Paul alone that killed the six hijackers. Isaack was so impressed he reached into one of the bags pulling out fifty thousand dollars for each man and sixty for Paul, giving each man a firm handshake as he handed over their rewards telling them to take a few days off and enjoy the money.

Paul drove home and immediately took a long shower, then lay naked on his couch thinking. "I am done." He thought to himself, with the weapons at the farm, the money, the link to the cartel. "Truly, they must have enough now!" he thought. The phone rang once and stopped. An hour later it rang again and stopped. Paul felt drained tonight, he just wanted to stay home and do nothing. The phone rang again and stopped, he knew it was Reese who was calling. He had not seen her or had any contact with her for ten days. He knew she was worried and decided to make the walk to her house. For some reason after he was dressed, Paul went to his closet and pulled out the Glock and dropped in a magazine, then placed it in the back of his pants. He had no reason to arm himself, he just for some reason wanted it.

   He left his apartment and walked directly to Reese's and knocked on the door. He could see Thomas sitting at the table drinking coffee through the window as he stood outside waiting for the door to open. Reese let him in giving him a big hug but not showing too much in front of Thomas. Paul walked in and Reese poured him a cup of coffee which he happily took then sat down, Reese and Thomas both took notepads and recorders for the debriefing.

   Paul told them the entire story from the start at the farm until he walked to the door of Reese's apartment. They looked at him in horror when he told them he had killed six gangsters in Chicago. "Six, Christ man," Thomas said surprised, while Reese assured him it was self defense and he would not be charged. He told them the names of the cartel guys he had befriended while they housed him in the body shop. The location of the weapons at the farm, but the most important thing he remembered was the name Havier had casually mentioned to him. "Grimes, the money man," with the fact that Havier had mentioned he was someone important to the cartel and was also connected to Isaack. Reese said she would look into it herself. Thomas began asking questions about anything he may have heard about the government contacts, but he had nothing more for him, Paul had given him all he knew and had nothing more to report.

"That is all I know buddy. Now you have enough Thomas, the weapons, the money, the cartel, the name of the money guy. I am out," Paul stated firmly, both Thomas and Reese looked at Paul nervously. Thomas shook his head and said,

"No, you are not done." Paul raised his hands in the air and when he started speaking his tone was of frustration.

"Yes, Thomas, I damn well am!" Thomas placed his pen and notepad on the table to try and talk sense into Paul.

"Paul, we need you to stay in a little longer and find out where the rest of the weapons are at and who is giving them info in the government." Paul was not having it,

"Listen, you can find that out when you arrest these assholes, someone will talk. I have given you hundreds of names of people to question. I am done!" Paul shouted and slammed his hand on the table. Reese walked over in front of him and knelt placing her hands on his leg.

"Paul, the Secretary of Defense Martin Sibley might be involved. We need you to stay in to try and confirm this and find his connection to Isaack." Thomas and Reese both said nothing as they watched Paul process this and let it sink in. Paul was not dumb, both Reese and Thomas knew this, they knew he would do what was right.

"This is some deep shit," Paul said with a fascinated tone.

"Sorry Paul, we could not tell you buddy," Thomas said to his friend hoping there was no hard feelings.

"It is fine," Paul replied.

Thomas looked at Reese kneeling on the floor in front of Paul, and something dawned on him like he was punched in the face.

"Reese, why are you being nice to him? You two are never nice to each other." Neither Paul or Reese said anything, but then Thomas started laughing and shouted. "Oh, my God! Are you two sleeping together?" And then he burst into laughter.

"I really should kick your ass!" Paul said threatening Thomas who was still laughing.

"Do us a favor and don't say anything," Paul asked Thomas, who nodded back. Thomas and Reese had a conversation about the information given to them by Paul, after they were done Thomas took his notes and left, leaving the two of them alone. As soon as Thomas had closed the door Paul walked over to Reese and pushed her against the wall and started to ravage her body.

"I was so worried about you, not hearing a word for ten days," Reese said as she pulled him close and felt the gun. Surprised, she stepped back looking at him.

"I killed six guys few days ago, I am feeling a little paranoid you know," Paul stated in defense of himself, and Reese smiled.

"I can arrest you for this Paul," she lectured smiling at him. Paul looked at her and putting on his best ghetto gangster voice said,

"Yea, well you can try bitch." Reese burst out laughing as she walked over taking the gun from him and setting it on the table, then returned to pulling off his clothes.

Chapter 18.

July 15th. Michigan near Lake Huron.

Paul had been driving the white Ford E-450 sixteen-foot cube van for hours, he was heading to the far eastern shore of Michigan. He could see Lake Huron to his right as he drove north, he was almost to Harbor Beach, and the GPS was telling him to turn left in one hundred yards. He followed the directions and turned into a farmer's yard where he could see Jones and Alfred waving him over to the large blue machinery shop with a white overhead door.

Paul pulled the van around back and parked it out of sight of the main road. Jones and Alfred were drinking coffee joking about how long it had taken Paul to get there. Alfred had been decent to Paul since they had gotten back from Chicago. Jones said it was because "Alfred is shit scared of you ever since you killed all those nigger hijackers in Chicago." Paul didn't care if Alfred liked him or not, he was just happy the kid wasn't being such an idiot to him anymore, the constant attitude was beginning to work on Paul's last nerve.

The farmer came out of his house walking quickly over to Paul and the other two bringing Paul a hot cup of coffee.

"Here you go son, I suspect you drove through the night too," The forty something farmer said as he handed him the hot cup. "I hope you like it black," he added.

"Thank you, Sir." Paul said politely then scanned the property, it was a beautiful piece of land right by the lake, lots of trees, horses in the corral and it was all well maintained. You could tell this man had pride in his home and worked hard to keep it up. Paul looked at the farmer and said, "I love your property, Sir. It is breath taking."

"It sure is. But it is not mine anymore. Some corporation has forced me out, so they can build a refinery here. Oh, they paid me going rate alright, but not a nickel for all the pride, and hard work I have put into this place ever since my mom and dad helped me buy it twenty-one years ago. This is my home, I built it, and I never would have sold it for any price, so they forced me out with honourless lawyers. A man cannot keep what he has worked for in this goddamn country anymore!" the farmer shouted in rage.

He then walked over to the shop and opened the overhead door. The shop was loaded with weapons, more than Paul would ever have thought possible. He saw dozens of crates containing Soviet made SA-7 surface to air man portable missiles, RPGs, lots of mines, explosives and over a hundred rifles with ridiculous amounts of rifle and light machine gun ammunition. Just the site of these weapons made Paul shiver, he truly did just realize the massive scale of Isaack's operation, so many weapons have come in and so many more have left here to other sites. If Isaack sets his plan in motion whatever it is, the entire nation could end up in flames.

Paul put on his best fake happy face and picked up an SA-7.

"How are you getting these?" Paul asked. Jones laughed at Paul,

"They come across Lake Huron from Canada," Jones bragged. Alfred then had to put his two cents in now,

"Yea, we got some good friends up there that work in the ports in Newfoundland. They just take them off the boats, load them on trucks and drive them on out of the port before they are inspected. Then they take them some place safe until water transport is ready, then load them on a boat, then they meet one of our boats out in the lake some place, transfer the weapons from boat to boat and boom they come here," Alfred explained. Paul set the SA-7 back down, then took a drink of his coffee. His stomach was upset from the nerves, and his mind was racing. "How many loads have come in?" Paul thought as his mind raced, "I will need to tell Reese this information, so she can phone the Mounties up there."

Paul, Jones and Alfred spent the morning loading the trucks with as much ordinance as they could get on board, but Paul's truck had to be loaded with a special order. Alfred and Jones would go back to Flint, but Paul was heading south this day, to Lima, Ohio. He had orders to meet Isaack and a few MLB members down there for a meeting with another group that Isaack was trying to recruit. After his truck was loaded, Paul said his goodbyes and jumped in. He made sure everything was strapped down proper and covered with tarps, so no one could easily see what he was hauling. Paul placed a magazine in a Makarov 9mm and put it in the inside pocket of his jacket. "I am not taking any chances after Chicago!" he said aloud making Jones laugh.

The drive to Lima took Paul a little over four hours, he met Isaack and some men outside of town at a gas station diner, after he parked the truck where it could be observed the entire time while they were inside the diner. Paul walked in and sat down looking at the old greasy spoon diner with the lunch counter and seating booths that should have been replaced about ten years ago. He smelled the burgers cooking and his stomach growled. He had not eaten all day. Then he sat down with Isaack, greeting him and his two escorts. Isaack smiled at Paul and said,

"I took the liberty of ordering for you Paul, I thought you probably had not eaten all day." "You're a good man sir," Paul said to him. The waitress brought the coffee pot by asking if he wanted one which he happily said, "Yes" to. They ate their burgers and fries while talking about bad politics and the corrupt politicians, no one spoke a word of business inside the crowded diner. After they were done Isaack paid the bill, and they walked outside. Isaack lit a cigarette as they all walked over to Paul's truck where Isaack began to explain. "We are meeting with the Ohio Citizen Guard tonight; their spineless leader Mark Clark is getting cold feet. He has accepted large amounts of money from us so he better change his mind. His second in command, Ernest Spaatz, is a good man and is well on board with us so they may be having a change of leadership tonight. Keep your eyes open anyway tonight Paul, Mr. Clark may have a few friends left in his crew." Paul nodded at Isaack, and when he finished explaining, Paul got in his truck and followed Isaack and his men to the meeting.

They met in a large open field behind a row of granaries and some farming equipment. Six men were waiting there for them, all of them were armed with a variety of different assault rifles and pistols, and all of them were visibly nervous. Isaack and his two escorts exited the ford Bronco. Isaack carried his Colt 1911 in his right hand and a cigarette in his left. Paul stepped out of the truck keeping himself back far enough away to keep an eye on the nervous men. Isaack greeted the OCG kindly with a nod, and then verbally to Clark himself. "Mr. Clark," Isaack said.

"Isaack," Mark Clark replied. Mark Clark was a fat man, unshaven for days and his clothes had not seen water for weeks by the looks of him. His black hair was tucked under a red and white ballcap and his belly stuck out from under his t-shirt. He stood in front of Isaack breathing heavily and sweating profusely with nervousness. There was silence all around them for a moment until Isaack tucked the Colt into his belt, then reached into his back pocket and pulled out a large envelope and offered it to Mark without saying a word. "No!" Mark stuttered. Isaack took a long drag on his cigarette, then dropped the butt to the ground and stepped on it.

"You took money from us Mark," Isaack said slowly, "with the commitment of joining us." He almost sounded scary, Paul thought while listening.

"Yes, but you guys are too wild for us! You will have us all in jail or dead!" Mark said accusingly.

It was then when another Ohio man stepped for forward,

"You're a goddamn coward Mark!" the man shouted nervously at Mark. Isaack smiled at the man's outburst.

"Hello Ernest, nice of you to get involved in your own coronation." Isaack said calmly. Ernest Spaatz was a twenty-nine-year-old mechanic, he did some time in prison for assault on a police officer, and when he came out of prison he had a strong hatred for the government. He was fit and kept himself well groomed, and not one of his brown hairs on his head was out of place. Mark looked at both men confused and emotional.

"What do you mean coronation?" Isaack raised an eyebrow at Ernest and dipped his head towards Mark giving Ernest the signal to talk.

"You're out Mark! I am taking the Guard from you," Ernest said sternly, Mark stood frozen in disbelief before screaming at Ernest.

"Like hell you are! You son of a bitch convict! That is what you are! A no-good convict!"

Mark began getting emotional and tightened his grip on the rifle he was carrying. Isaack lit another cigarette and placed the lighter into his right front pants pocket and when he pulled his hand out of his pocket he casually grabbed the Colt 1911 and brought it up to Mark's face and pulled the trigger. The loud shot put everyone in the area into shock and Isaack tucked the gun back into his belt again, then handed the envelope to Ernest. Everyone stood silent, and just stood looking at Mark laying dead on the ground.

Isaack stepped over Mark's corpse and addressed the remaining members.

"You all work for me now. Tow the line, or Mark will have some company. We aim to change this country and you can be apart of it or die with it! For it does not matter to me if you all die. The rewards for loyalty will be great," Isaack preached to them, then called to Paul. "Paul give them the keys," Paul walked over and gave Ernest the keys to the truck, then turned and walked back to the Bronco. Isaack was climbing in the Bronco, but then stopped and shouted to Ernest. "Oh, Ernest, hide the body proper and bring the truck back when you are done please, the weapons are all there. We are going to change the world." Paul could not believe just how relaxed Isaack was after he just flat out murdered a man in cold blood.

The drive home took the rest of the night, and it was early morning before they got back to Paul's truck. He immediately got inside and turned the key, but before he could drive away Isaack walked over and banged on the hood getting Paul's attention. "Come see me tomorrow." Isaack shouted. Paul gave him a thumb up as he drove away thinking of what a true psychotic, madman Isaack Elzey really was.

Chapter 19.

July 16. Washington D.C. J. Edgar Hoover building.

Reese sat in front of Director Bryant's desk silent as Bryant had his head resting in both of his palms cursing silently. "He killed six? A shootout in daylight in the middle of Chicago, and he killed six of the hijackers with a smuggled AK-47? This after he burned down a church and set up a man to be killed by the police?" Bryant asked softly. Director Cromwell and Thomas Price were both present in the room. Director Cromwell was smiling at Bryant, when Bryant noticed his smile he shrugged at Cromwell who laughingly said,

"Remember when you laughed at me over the Congressional hearings for the drone strikes? Well, I cannot wait to see you on the hot seat on T.V. for this one," then clapped his hands and grinned. Bryant found no humor in this,

"You will be right there beside me!" he snapped defensively. Cromwell laughed harder stating,

"How? I am a spy. I was never here," clapping his hands again as Bryant held up his middle figure to Cromwell.

"Alright, back to business," Bryant ordered then smiled shaking his head at Cromwell who snickered at him again. Reese then continued her briefing, "After Paul defended himself in Chicago, he returned to the body shop where he and his team were protected by the cartel. A doctor was brought in and treated the Vos brother. During this time, Paul was talking to a mid ranking cartel

member named Havier, Havier let the name of a money man slip, that the cartel
bosses might be angry with them for losing the bags of money." Reese opened a bottle of water and took a drink. Bryant and Cromwell listened carefully impatiently waiting for her to finish.

"Then Paul returned to Flint and reported the money man's name to me as a Mr. Grimes. Having no knowledge of this man, and not wanting to use FBI resources like you said, I thought of the cartel affiliation, so I contacted the DEA, sir," she explained, looking at Bryant who was eating this up.

"Okay," he said, then Reese continued, "The DEA knew exactly who he was, all I said was the name "Grimes" and they told me almost everything from memory. His name is Bryan Grimes owner of Grimes Financial, he is an American living in Switzerland." Reese continued with her briefing on Grimes and his suspected dealing with the cartels and other organized crime groups.

When Reese was done both agency directors were extremely impressed. Cromwell finally put some knowledge into the meeting.

"I believe we should send someone over to Zurich and have a talk with this man Grimes and by chat, I mean beat the crap out of him or maybe a little waterboarding. You know, just until he talks!" Cromwell stated, disgusted with the profile of Grimes. Bryant sat back down angry again.

"Who? We are being watched, remember?" Bryant said frustrated. Thomas then spoke up,

"Us, me and Reese. We go as a couple and fly commercial at our own expense. Reese takes some holiday time, tells everyone she is going to Zurich with her new... handsome boyfriend... Me." Thomas boasted jokingly, "We book one room, then go knock on this guy's door, or make a meeting by telling him we are money people for, I don't know, some rich people." The two directors listened carefully to Thomas then agreed that this would be a good plan, and both quickly approved.

Thomas now asked for a moment to brief them on something new, "We all know that President Shuisky has asked for a prisoner exchange for Fedir Osetsky." Both men answered,

"Yes." Then Bryant spoke up, "and that son of a bitch Martin Sibley is asking to speed the transfer up, can you believe that? The boldness of that bastard!" Then he apologized to Thomas and asked him to carry on. Thomas smiled and took a deep breath,

"We have a line on Fedir's wife Shura. We know for a fact that she has been the main force in the movement of the weapons to the MLB," Thomas explained, hoping for a reaction out of the room but nothing came. "Reliable intel says that Shura Osetsky will be in the coastal city of Merca, Somalia in two days for a meeting with some warlord asshole over some weapons. I had a team in Yemen taking care of... well taking care of something is all I can say," Thomas said realizing some things they were still doing for the CIA could not be spoken of. Cromwell nodded at Thomas in thanks for catching himself. Then Thomas continued his briefing, "I have a team in route by sea, we bummed a ride from a fellow PMC company that we have worked with in the past. These guys are pirate hunters and owed us one or two favors, they are under contract by several shipping companies to provide security for the shipping lanes. My team will be dropped off and Zodiac in and we are going to grab that evil bitch," Thomas said smiling. Cromwell was listening intensely and spoke up curiously.

"Thomas, what assets do you have for support in this area?" he asked.

"Just my team going in sir," Thomas said, knowing what was coming from Cromwell next.

"So, if the shit goes bad, what happens to your men?" The risk is there Sir, but my men volunteered for this one, no one was ordered. They want her as bad as you do. The hotel she will be in is only four hundred yards from the water sir. In and out," Thomas added, defending his plan.

"Well, they are your men," Cromwell said wit a little concern.

Chapter 20.

July 17. Flint, Michigan.

Paul walked up to Isaack's large home and knocked on the door, he was wearing the tiger strip camo he had been issued after being accepted as a brother to the MLB. Paul also carried the Glock that was once his father's, it was strapped to his right hip along with two full mags in pouches on his left hip. He also wore the black beret with a fabric patch sewn on the front with the image of one shackled fist with a dangling broken chain. Everyone had been issued one of these berets and told to wear it only with their uniforms. Wearing this completed uniform strangely gave Paul the feeling of legitimacy, like he was a real solider again with a shameful feeling of pride as he kept it clean and pressed.

Isaack pulled a curtain to the side, then pointed for Paul to follow the deck around to the back, which he did. Paul pulled a chair out at the patio table and sat down taking in a deep breath of the fresh country air, then let it out quickly letting his shoulders slump down.

Isaack walked out with two cups of coffee and sat down, "You take it black, right?" Isaack asked politely.

"That is fine, sir, thank you," Paul said politely taking the cup directly to his lips. "Fine morning," Paul said placing the cup back down on the table. Isaack lit a cigarette then leaned back in the chair with his cup in the other hand.

"Well, about last night?" Isaack asked curiously as he looked at Paul. Paul looked Isaack in the eyes and replied,

"What about it?" Like last night was no big deal. "We murdered a man Paul. How does that make you feel?" Isaack asked, looking at Paul and staring into Paul's eyes like he could read his mind.

"A man like that clearly could not be trusted with what he knew. After being demoted by his crew the fat tub would probably run to the police. I don't feel like you had a choice," Paul explained calmly. Isaack seemed to buy it and seemed to relax as he took another drink of his coffee. Paul looked at Isaack, he felt like this was the best time he had since he got inside the MLB to get some information from Isaack. Another opportunity with Isaack like this where he was trusting Paul may never return. "Isaack, everyone seems to know what the master plan is but me. Have I not proven myself?" Paul knew this was a risk but took it. Isaack smiled looking at Paul.

"Well Paul, I guess you have. I am sure you know from your military time that keeping a secret is hard." Paul nodded in agreement and Isaack took another drag from his smoke, then continued. "All I can say is that within six months we will pull off the greatest military action against this nation since Pearl Harbor. What we do will change this nation forever and plunge it into civil war. The economy will shut down and anarchy will cover the nation. We will retake control of the nation with force and kindness. We have people in ranking positions in the government ready to take control. I will not lead the nation Paul, but I will make sure it is run properly." Paul looked at Isaack frustrated, he knew the same now that he did before Isaack's speech.

"I have heard you and few others talking of committing the ACT, and when it is completed the remaining militias around the nation will be inspired and rise up with you," Paul pressed. Isaack paused before answering Paul.

"There is less than thirty people who know the answer to that Paul. When the time comes for the act to commence, the followers of the thirty will follow or die, they will be told moments before we attack so they will not be able to endanger the mission. We have over a thousand members now bearing arms, a thousand people cannot be trusted to hold a secret of this magnitude." Isaack looked Paul in the eyes again. "We will take the head off the government, not just politicians Paul, but everyone who works for them. The President who acts like a KING, will die in the White House he treats like a PALACE! We have a man inside ready to legally take his throne after the streets of Washington run red with blood."

Paul sat horrified at what Isaack had just told him. Paul knew it was too dangerous to push anymore, and Paul thought that Isaack was not only a fucking psychopath, he was smart, and Paul knew when to stop pushing, so he said nothing else. Isaack took another drink of coffee then looked into Paul's eye's again. "Well boy?" Isaack said, waiting for a response from Paul.

"Well, they have been warned over the years, I guess they have been warned enough," Paul replied. Isaack reached into his pocket and tossed Paul another envelope full of cash, smiling,

"A new world," Isaack shouted. Paul sat looking at Isaack fighting the urge to shoot him in the head right then and there.

Chapter 21.

July 19. Off the coast of Merca, Somalia.

Tim O'Brien kept his body low in the Zodiac this night as he had his team inserted into the beach to Merca, a city on the coast of Somalia. His M-4 with the M203 grenade launcher attachment felt good in his hands this night. It had been some time since he had some real action and part of him craved a good fight. They had been dropped off three miles out to sea by a fellow PMC company doing them a favor by giving them a ride, then sitting out there waiting for their return. Tim turned on his GPS checking his approach and they were spot on target. Tim was leading sixteen men this night and they thanked God that there was no moon. He pressed his push to talk (PTT) for his radio, which was attached to his tac vest letting the team know they were one minute off the beach.

Tim's tactical communication headset was set on two COMM channels: one to his team and the other to the CIG headquarters in Maryland. Thomas Price was sitting in the situation room right now with the two ex-JAG lawyers who owned CIG, and probably several other people would be present as well. The right earpiece in Tim's headset came to life as his sixteen-man team acknowledged his transmission. Over the left Thomas's voice was then heard.

"Good luck boys." Tim was wishing he had more men for this mission, not to mention some air support. Going into Somalia with sixteen men was,

163

well, fucking suicidal he thought. But it was a short notice mission and Shura Osetsky would not be here long so, sometimes a risk was worth it. Well, that is what the lawyers told him anyway. His team was solid, numerous ex-Marine Force Recon, Rangers, four Seals, and a couple Green Berets and three former SAS guys, one who was an Australian that was crazy as shit named Cyril Norman. Cyril loved action, but not too much that it impaired his professionalism. He was short, maybe five feet nine on a good day, but tough as Hell. Many years on the rugby field gave him a toughness that most operators dreamed of. His downfall Tim always thought was his hair, he had too much and that gave him a look of a Viking. CIG only hired the best and if that meant taking men in from other nations then so be it, after all, Tim was a Canadian. They had worked and trained together long enough that they had developed into one of the best private military units in the world, and back in Maryland, Thomas was wishing like Hell he was with them.

"NVGs on," Tim told his team and pulled down his AN/PVS-14-night vision and he could immediately see the beach coming closer. The man driving the Zodiac lifted the engine allowing them to get closer and every man jumped off the boat except the two who stayed with the Zodiacs taking them back out to sea a few hundred yards. As they ran off the beach Tim dropped an infrared strobe marker on the sand, so the boatmen could hold position using their NVGs to see the flash. Once they cleared the sand they stopped and rechecked their position. "Now, where is that bitch?" Tim said silently while checking his GPS. She was not far away and was less than four hundred yards inland, but four hundred yards through a city where everyone and their goddamn grandmother packs an AK and is well motivated to kill them, is a hell of a long way.

Tim pressed the PTT for the command channel. "Snatch One to Central Station. We are moving to target location now," Tim reported.
"Central Station, Roger that, good hunting brother. I wish I was with you," Thomas replied. Tim used hand signals and the men moved out silently as they left the beach heading inland. Shura was only going to be here in Merca for the remainder of the night, she was here making another weapons deal with some douche bag warlord and his pirate asshole buddies. Tim had never shot a pirate before, maybe tonight would be the night because, well, that would be cool. The informant said she was accompanied by four guards and one aide. The rest of the security was the responsibility of her hosts.

"Thank God there is no moon," Tim said into the team channel.

"Yea, movement has been good so far," one of the former SAS members replied. The street was filthy, garbage littered it everywhere and burned-out cars lined much of the street, Tim did not mind as they made good cover. The old houses with their flat roofs seemed to be the only type of building around this area. They took a direct line down the darkened back street, this part of the world had little use for street lights, which was making things easy for the team. Tim lead Snatch, one who took the point, while Cyril quietly brought up Snatch Two fifty yards behind.

They had made it in record time through the city without seeing a soul. Tim brought Snatch one to a stop, they had the target building in sight now. It was not hard to find as it was the only three-story hotel in sight for many blocks in each direction, not to mention the first building to have lights on since they had left the beach. Tim spread his men out in a large walled off lot on the opposite side of the street that was filled with several Masala fruit trees. The men lined up against the wall laying low out of sight. He radioed Snatch two and told Cyril they were at their designated spot.

Tim lifted his NVGs to take a look in the dim light. The building was a very old three-story hotel that the owner did what he could to keep it up and had made a little money in the process. It was almost entirely made from concrete and had a flat roof. One entrance on the side facing Tim and Snatch one and another in the back for staff. Snatch two had a sniper and a saw gunner on his left flank covering that side from his side of the street. There were two armed guards with AKs on duty at the front door, with another at the back, plus they had no idea how many were inside.

Snatch Two made their way one block farther down the street and crossed over bringing themselves up kiddy corner to Snatch One's position.

"Snatch Two to Snatch One. We are in position mate, but just to let you know out back here there are seven armed technicals parked down the street approx. three zero meters," Cyril informed Tim.

"Roger Two, keep an eye on them, we are sending in the rabbits now," Tim replied, then pointed at two men in his team. They were both black, one was a former Marine and the other a Green Beret who could speak the lingo here fluently.

"Sucks to fit the local profile," the Marine quietly said as they stripped off their gear placing everything into their packs, then donned the local attire they had brought with them. Each placed a Heckler & Koch EX–23 with a sound suppressor into their clothing out of sight. Both men shoved a cell phone into the pocket with a wad of cash, then made their way back towards the beach a block, then returning from another angle.

Tim pressed the PTT when he saw the two rabbits crossing the street to the hotel.

"Snatch One to Central Station, rabbits entering the hole," Thomas acknowledged him with a single,

"Roger." The two rabbits walked up to the two guards and began conversing, it only took them a half minute and they were allowed entry. Tim waited impatiently, his hands felt tired from gripping his M-4 so hard. Tim suddenly got a strange feeling in his stomach, like this is such a bad idea being here, but he always felt this way after he sent his friends into a messed-up situation.

He tried relaxing as he watched the front doors and waited but was unable to with his friends in the hotel. Six minutes to the second had passed when both men came walking out of the hotel. Their pace was considerably faster than what it was on their way in, but still they tried to make it look casual. A second later the hotel door opened again, and a white male walked out standing with the guards watching them walk away, then five more armed black males followed him out. The white man studied them walking away closely, even from across the street Tim could make out the concern on his face. Then he began shouting something, Tim did not speak the language, so he did not know what he was shouting. Tim felt it, that moment in your mind, that instant less than one second before you know the shit is going to hit the fan. Cyril must have felt it too because over the radio came a,

"Fuck mate!" Then Tim keyed his radio,

"Snatch One to all Snatch call signs. If any of them raises a weapon go hot!" The white man yelled again, but the two Snatch members ignored him and kept walking. Tim thought he sounded Russian, but he was not sure. He readied his M-4, placing it to his shoulder and sighting on the soon to be dead nine gunmen standing at front door of the hotel. The white man was holding an Israeli made Uzi. He lifted the weapon with one hand and pointed it at Tim's men who had now crossed the street. As he raised the Uzi, Tim was not about to wait another second and he opened up with his M-4. The white man instantly dropped on the stairs dead. The sound of the gunfire caused the other seven guards to at first, stand there staring in shock, then look for cover. A half a dozen teammates opened up on the guards, dropping them all in a few seconds.

The two rabbits came running back to Tim's position, putting on their vests and picking up their gear.

"Tim, we got to go!" one of them yelled.

"What about the target?" Tim asked.

"She is there, but so is a warlord or someone special with half his fucking crew!" A second later half the windows in the hotel began getting smashed out one at a time, and rifle barrels came out raining down Hell on the position of Snatch one.

Tim was a smart soldier, and knew the mission was over, he keyed his COMM unit,

"Snatch One to all units, move back to the beach now!" And after a few quick acknowledgments the team began moving back in good order. As the team began moving back, Snatch One kept position until Snatch Two had crossed back across the street, and in that short time twenty men came charging out of the hotel. More were coming from down the street where the warlord had his vehicles parked. They came running down the street without any discipline firing wildly as they moved. Snatch Two was making their way one block south parallel with Snatch One but were not under fire.

Tim and the rest of Snatch one were quickly retreating in good order firing effective cover fire for their teammates as they moved. This fire was slowing down the mad men charging at them firing entire magazines with one squeeze of the trigger.

Tim could hear something else and the place began to light up as the headlights of four Toyota trucks also known as a technical began to light up the street. Each had a large caliber machine gun mounted in the back and all four were firing indiscriminately into the walls of the houses the team was using as cover. Tim stepped out and with his M203 launcher lobbed a 40mm grenade directly beside the lead Toyota causing it to burst into flames killing the three men inside and giving them a momentary break as most of the men shooting at them stopped firing. All Snatch One members used this few seconds to gain some distance from the other vehicles before they recovered from the confusion.

They made it halfway to the beach before the second technical caught up again, and the man in the back was firing at them wildly. Tim pushed the

PTT. "We need to take out these guys or we will be unable to evac on the boats!" he said as he let another grenade go from his M203, which landed beside the technical and exploded. Their retreat had stopped, and a fire fight had started as the rest of the men from the hotel caught up with their buddies in the Toyotas and opened fire on them.

Thomas listened to a report from Tim and slammed his fist on the boardroom table causing the two lawyers to jump in their chairs.

"Get to the beach god damn it!" Tim yelled into the radio and was just about to move when he noticed on his left flank an incredible rate of fire on the enemy that a second before was firing at Snatch one. Snatch two had made their way close unseen to their brother's aid and were putting the hurt on the Somalians. As soon as the last technical was silenced, Tim ordered Snatch one to move forward towards the remaining enemy who were still on foot and were directing all their attention on Snatch two and not paying any attention to Snatch one who was right behind them. Tim gave the order to advance, and the order was followed and with the speed of the most seasoned, talented warriors Snatch one advanced aggressively firing in a controlled calm as they moved killing the remaining enemies.

"Report, anyone hit?" Tim asked into the radio. One man called out asking for assistance. Cyril had been struck by a bullet which went in the meat on his upper arm and came out without hurting anything important. Tim ran over to him as his men helped him to his feet and they began making their way to the beach. "Oh muffin, are you going to be okay?" Tim asked sarcastically.

"Shut up! You prick!" Cyril shouted at him. The team quickly made the run to the beach where both boats were waiting for them at the strobe.

"Sounded like you guys had some fun," one of the boatmen said.

"Yep, total cluster fuck!" Tim said frustrated, then shouted to the team.

"Let's go, more are coming." They could hear the engines of vehicles coming as well as shouting from the city as it began to stir from the noise of the fight. They climbed in the Zodiacs and once it was confirmed they had everyone, they began moving out to sea. The ocean was getting a little rough as the wind had picked up, and several fighters were now on the shoreline looking out to sea trying to find them, and some fired into the darkness. A technical pulled up with a browning .50 Cal mounted in the back and immediately began spraying the darkness in hopes he could hit something. The skinny man firing was shooting blind into the darkness not knowing where they were as he raked back and forth, but more than once it came close. Once the man firing it stopped to reload, Tim told the boatman to stop the engine. He reached over and grabbed his drag bag he had decided to leave in the Zodiac when they were heading inland and retrieved his scoped M-14 with composite stock and popped the lens covers off the optics. They were seven hundred yards away, the fires from the burning Toyotas silhouetted the five men standing around the newly arrived technical perfectly. Tim lay across the body of the Zodiac lengthways and slowed his breathing. The water rocked the boat, Tim breathed carefully and watched the man reloading the Browning, then pulled the bolt back swinging it to the ocean again and prepared to fire. Tim placed the crosshairs on the man's heart and waited for the boat to bob downward again and pulled the trigger. The man in the back of the Toyota fell backwards out of the truck box onto the ground. He then placed the optic on the next man and three seconds later he squeezed the trigger again, making him drop lifeless like the first one. The remaining men turned and fled the beach, but not before another was struck in the back of the head with another round from Tim's rifle. He then sat back down in the boat.

"Let's go!" he told the driver and they headed out to sea again. Tim keyed his radio. "Snatch One to Central Station. Snatch units are safe, and water bound, one wounded not bad, headed to Black Beard, over." Thomas breathed a sigh of relief.

"Central Station, roger. Sorry boys," Thomas said hoping the beating they might give him when he got home was not going to be too bad, then realized he and Reese had to catch a plane first thing in the morning for Zurich and smiled when he looked at the two lawyers sitting behind him talking. "Good, they can deal with the team when they come home pissed off."

Chapter 22.

July 27. Zurich, Switzerland.

Thomas and Reese waited days in Zurich before being granted a meeting with Bryan Grimes. Grimes Financial had offices in seven cities around the world, but Grimes himself only conducted business out of his home. He had private security guards twenty-four hours a day and a steady stream of people coming and going from his high-end home. Somehow Reese had convinced one of Grimes's underlings she was a representative of a corporation looking for Grimes Financials' African connections to reopen a mining operation that could be worth billions.

"You can sure spin a line of bullshit, Reese," Thomas said approvingly to her as they pulled up to the gatehouse in front of his massive hilltop villa. The guard checked their identification to his list of approved appointments, then allowed them access. Thomas drove the rented black BMW up to the front doors and was surprised to find there was even valet parking. They were escorted inside by a butler who seated them in a private library which doubled as a waiting room. Thomas was trying to figure a way of pressuring Grimes into talking, interviewing criminals was not something he had much experience in. His only experience in interrogating he learned in the army, and his first choice of interrogation tactics was water boarding, but with Grimes' armed security in the house, that was out. Neither he or Reese were armed, which further complicated things.

Thomas walked around the private library reading the bindings on the books, he had not heard of any of them before. Reese had found an old classic and was patiently glancing through it before the butler returned. Asking them to follow him, he led them up a flight of stairs and down a long hallway to a door, but before entering the office, they were both searched for listening devices and weapons. When the security guard was satisfied, they were allowed to enter the office. Grimes sat behind a large stone carved desk that Thomas guessed was marble. His office even looked like what one would expect some asshole billionaire's would. A large six-foot square painting of Napoleon hung on one wall, and a bust of Julius Caesar was placed against another. A suit of armour, and numerous antique weapons were placed on display around the room. The floor was shinny black tile and two brown leather couches sat in the middle facing each other. Thomas felt afraid to touch anything, afraid he might break something.

Grimes sent the butler away keeping only one very good looking female brunette aide with them who sat with pen and paper ready to take notes. Introductions were made and so far, Reese had done all the talking, "Well what can we do for each other?" Grimes said, sitting down crossing his fingers as he rested hands on the desk. Reese sat looking at Grimes not saying a word, he looked at her and Thomas both then uncrossed his fingers raising his palms upwards. "Hello?" Grimes said in an attempt to get one of them to talk. Reese then leaned forward on her chair and began dropping a bomb on Grimes,

"Mr. Grimes, I am not a financial representative for a mining corporation. I am an FBI agent, my name is special agent Reese Gilbert and I am here to tell you sir, that as of this minute the United States of America is going to spend every resource we have seizing all your accounts, assets and make your life a living Hell. We will also be under the Patriot Act, charging you with ties to terrorist organizations. Have you ever heard of Guantanamo Bay? Well, sir, we have worse places than that, Mr. Grimes and you qualify for a cell in one of them. Thomas almost fell out of his chair, "What the hell was she doing?" Thomas thought. "She is already giving up why we were here." Thomas looked at the aide who was listening to this with a blank look on her face. She looked at Thomas who placed his figure over his lips, and the aide just looked down uncomfortably at her notepad. Grimes' smile had left his face and his mouth hung open as he sat there in his chair frozen. Reese went on telling him that they had evidence linking financial transactions to a Mexican cartel. Thomas then realized she was bluffing him, and even bluffed so hard as to tell him they had proof he was moving money around for a known weapons dealer who was sending weapons into the United States for terrorist activities. She went on telling him what the penalties would be when they get him back on U.S. soil and she assured him that they would be getting him.

Reese stopped talking then and just stared at Grimes, who was looking like he was going to have a massive stroke. Thomas looked at Grimes, then at Reese, "Damn that girl is scary when she wants to be," he thought. Grimes looked at his aide and politely asked her to leave the room, which she happily did. Grimes waited for the door to close then nervously asked,

"You say you have proof?" Reese sternly replied,

"Yes, we have proof. Once you entered into the realm of supporting terrorism, you entered a whole new world." Grimes tried regaining his composure,

"This is ridiculous! I have not done anything illegal. My lawyers will..." Thomas leaned forward and slapped his hand on the stone desk and shouted,

"Shura Osetsky!" As soon as Grimes heard that name he went silent again. Thomas stood and walked over to the chair the aide had been sitting at, he knew Grimes was nervous and could see the anxiety pouring out of him. He moved the chair over closer to Grimes and sat down staring at him hard. "I am not an FBI agent, she is, but I am not. I am a different kind of agent for a different kind of agency." Grimes sat shaking, then opened the top drawer of his desk. Thomas looked making sure he was not pulling out a gun and he wasn't, but he pulled out a bottle of pills and quickly took one out placing it under his tongue. After a minute, Grimes began nervously talking,

"What…. what do you want from me?" he squeaked out. Thomas stood up and moved away from Grimes trying not to laugh and thinking what a pathetic loser Grimes was, and how easily Reese got him to break.

"You will answer every question I have for you today! You will provide me any records pertaining to the questions I have for you immediately. Failure to provide me with any of this information will result in the hammer!" Reese's voice was stern and came off like she was angry. "If you run from us we will find you. We found Saddam and we found Osama. So, finding you will be easy!" She explained in a very harsh manner. Grimes had become extremely emotional and a tear rolled down his cheek.

"Okay, anything you need, but I want immunity," Grimes pleaded. Thomas then spoke up yelling.

"No deals! Not until you help us Grimes! We will not allow you to tell us a bunch of bullshit and have nothing pan out! Cash in hand motherfucker!" Reese looked at Thomas giving him a look like maybe that was too much. Grimes was now full on weeping,

"Okay, but I will need to be protected," he choked out. Reese told him he will be protected and even offered him permission to bring a portion of his fortune with him into hiding. Thomas knew she never had the authority to offer any deals, but she was getting it done and he now knew what Paul saw in her. Reese reached into her briefcase and pulled out a small laptop and opened it. She entered the password and opened a file, then reached into the bag and pulled out a bright blue flash drive with a USB hookup for a computer and tossed it to Grimes. Reese then stood and walked over to Grimes and sat in the chair that Thomas had moved over beside him.

"Bryan, you will be protected. I can move you to the embassy tonight where no one will be able to touch you, then you will be moved back home on an Air Force plane under guard and placed into witness protection. But first you need to put all the files you have on Shura Osetsky and everything else relating to the weapons moving into the States on that flash drive I just gave you." Thomas watched how calm she was now and how Grimes calmed down when she looked him in the eyes and smiled.

Grimes said nothing. He just stood up and walked over to a section of wood paneling on the wall and started feeling along the trim and pulled open a panel exposing a safe. As Grimes started pushing the numbers on the touch pad entering the combination, Thomas quickly walked over and stood beside him making sure he was not going to pull out a gun. As Grimes opened the door Thomas could indeed see a gun. Grimes reached into the safe, and Thomas reached as well, taking Grimes by the wrist and pulling his hand out and twisting his hand around making Grimes' fingers point at his own face and applied pressure, lots of pressure. Grimes fell to his knees and cried out in pain.

"The laptop." Grimes muttered, "I was reaching for the laptop." Thomas let him go and stepped over to the safe and looked in it. Under the CZ-75 there was a laptop, Thomas reached in a retrieved it and handed it to Grimes.

"Sorry buddy. Nervous in the service right." Thomas said as he reached in and retrieved the gun checking to see if it was loaded, which it was, then placed it into his belt in the back of his pants.

Grimes took the laptop over to his desk and logged on. He began going over records with Reese on transfers to Shura and the cartel accounts, then transferred each of them to Reese's flash drive, then he showed her accounts in the United States that he had arranged cash and credit cards for.

An hour went by and Thomas had raided Grimes' wall bar finding a beer in the fridge and began drinking it, he was no use here, they were talking that educated language that he did not understand. Reese, she spoke it fine with her USC law degree, Thomas watched her, taking it all in and that impressed him. There was one question though that Thomas wanted to know which he was not sure if she had asked him yet.

"Hey," Thomas cut in and both looked at him as he crushed the Heineken can and tossed it at the garbage can beside Grimes' desk. "Maybe I missed it, but you are showing her where all this money has been going to, right? So just for my own piece of mind, where did it all come from?" Grimes looked at Paul and began getting nervous again, and Reese looked at Thomas with the look on her face of why the Hell did I not think to ask that myself look. Grimes never said a word. He just opened a folder on his laptop, and Reese looked at the screen for at least two minutes without blinking. Then she looked at Thomas and said,

"We need to phone Washington now!" She took the laptop from Grimes and began transferring files over to the flash drive herself. She began to look scared and she seemed to be in a hurry as well. Thomas began feeling her tension and sat upright instead of lounging,

"What is it?" Thomas asked her,

"The Russians," she said.

"Russians?" Thomas asked her not really following, then asked her again. Grimes then spoke up.

"A Russian FSB operative name Boris Donsky who has a personal relationship with Russian President Shuisky gave me billions almost four years ago, one of which was payment to me to set the financial side of this." Thomas feeling frustrated yelled,

"Set what up? What do the Russian have to do with this?" Grimes raised his hands up to Thomas and started talking to Thomas like he was a child.

"Okay, listen to me, Boris got billions from President Shuisky and gave it to me. Then he got Fedir Osetsky and several other weapons smugglers to begin to move weapons to a radical group back home in Michigan known as the Michigan Light Brigade. He used a contact he had from when the contact worked in Russia at the U.S embassy, now the same contact has moved up high in the government. I do not know who he is but one man that works for him, his name is Costner." Reese was writing everything down on her laptop as he spoke. Grimes continued talking to Thomas as if he was a child. "So then Costner is a go between for his boss and Boris who turned him somehow back when he was in Moscow at the Embassy. So, whoever the boss is in the States, goes to some guy he knows in the MLB and sets up this link giving them weapons and money." Thomas then interrupted and asked, "But why? Why do the Russians want to spend billions arming some retarded radical hillbillies?" Grimes smiled and explained,

"Think about it, if America is embroiled in a civil war, how much support will they be able to give Eastern Europe when the great Russian bear takes back all they lost after the fall of the Berlin wall?" Thomas and Reese both sat looking at Grimes wondering if he had more to say, but before he could answer questions there was a gunshot outside the building. Then another and another and then a burst of automatic fire. "The Russians!" Grimes cried out scared and reached into his desk pulling out a remote control and turned on the large television that hung on the wall. Thomas looked at Grimes and asked surprised,

"Russians? Here?" Grimes ignored him and pressed another button and it showed every camera on his property in small six-inch squares on the giant screen. Thomas looked at the screen, then pointed to the square showing the front door. Grimes turned that screen on large just in time to see four men burst through the front doors wearing masks and carrying MP-5s, killing the butler and anyone else they could see.

"Oh, I get it, the Russians are here!" Thomas said sarcastically as he pulled out the CZ-75 and racked the slide placing a round in the pipe as alarms began sounding throughout the house.

The masked men immediately headed up the stairs coming for the office they were in. More gunfire was heard, and Grimes cried out in horror as they killed his last bodyguard in the hallway outside his door. Thomas pushed one of the couches in front of the door, then walked over behind the stone carved desk and knelt. "Is there another hidden door in the wall like the safe?" Thomas asked Grimes who said nothing, he just jumped up and ran to the Napoleon painting and pulled it open revealing an entrance to a safe room. "Really?" Thomas said disbelievingly. Reese yelled for Grimes to get inside the saferoom, but Grimes ignored her and ran back to his desk picking up his laptop. Reese was packing her laptop and placed the flash drive into her bra.

Both he and Reese began rushing to the safe room when the gunmen in the hallway began spraying the room through the wall. Grimes took one of the first rounds fired in the temple and fell to the floor dead. Thomas dropped to the floor behind the stone desk, then returned two rounds back through the wall.

Reese had dropped to the floor and was crawling to Grimes picking up his laptop, once she retrieved it, she began moving to the safe room. Thomas stayed in place and screamed at Reese to close the door. She refused, then called for him to run to her. One of the men was pushing on the door, the couch began to slide on the tiled floor, Thomas fired one round into the door and ducked down again as another burst of fire came through the wall and smashed out the window behind him. Reese looked at Thomas and started crying, she slowly pulled the door closed, Thomas could see it on her face she knew he was going to die, but she had to save the information they had found. "Good girl," Thomas said aloud.

The men in the hallway had stopped firing as they were changing magazines, Thomas could hear the familiar sounds of empty magazines hitting the floor, he recognized it from years as a soldier. He stood, ran to the broken windows and dove out falling two stories down into some six-foot-high shrubs. They broke his fall, but left him tangled in the branches. He fought to get free and to catch his breath. He managed to get loose from the shrubs just as one of the masked gunmen began shooting at him from the window. Thomas dove and rolled behind a small three-foot-high stone wall in the garden. He took a fast look to the windows and the man was not there anymore. Thomas assumed the prick was coming back down the stairs after him. Not wanting to wait for him, he stood up and ran to the front of the house. "I am not trapped now motherfuckers!" Thomas quietly said to himself.

He was angry and even though Reese was locked in the safe room they may know a way inside. He knew he needed to kill the gunmen and quickly made his way around to the front of the house, just as one of the attackers came running out the front door. Thomas let two quick shots go with both hitting the man in the forehead, and he instantly fell to the ground dead. Thomas took a hold of the man and pulled him away from the door. He unslung the German made MP-5 the attacker was carrying and slung it over his own shoulder. He searched the body and found two more full magazines and a flash bang grenade.

He loaded up with the dead man's weapons, checked the MP-5 and began moving towards the front doors. He crept up looking in the open door slowly, seeing the entrance to the library and ran for it. He was less than three feet inside the room before he was being shot at by someone from up the stairs. Thomas was forced to dive and slide through the doorway on the hardwood floor to avoid being shot. Once inside the library he quickly stood and quietly moved to the wall next to the doorway and listened. He held his breath to hear any sound, nothing. He listened more and then he heard the distant sound of a magazine being removed from a weapon. Without thinking Thomas stepped into the doorway with the MP-5 tight to his shoulder. He scanned the stairwell from left to right, in less than a second, he saw the man who was just shooting at him placing a fresh magazine into his weapon and in less than another second Thomas put a three-round burst into the man's chest, causing him to drop to the floor and roll down the stairs. Just to be certain Thomas nailed him again.

Thomas then moved up the stairs, he could hear the remaining two men yelling in Russian beating on the safe room door. In any language, it does not matter if you can speak it or not, when someone is frustrated because he made a bad mistake and was going to be in some shit from his boss, that tone is international and these two idiots needed in that safe room desperately and they were not paying attention to the rest of the house. Thomas walked up to the office door and took a quick look inside. Both men were still yelling in Russian, while desperately kicking at the safe room door. Thomas pulled out the flashbang and pulled the pin on the Defensive Technologies 12-gram low roll flashbang and threw it into the room on a high arc at the safe room door. It hit the top of the door and bounced downwards hitting the floor, then bounced directly up again as it detonated leaving both men stunned and confused. Thomas entered the room as soon as he heard the bang, and with the MP-5 tight to his shoulder, he let four quick bursts loose killing both men easily.

Thomas walked over and gently knocked on the door while he called to Reese that it was safe to come out, but he was not sure if she could hear him or not. He then went over and began to inspect one of the dead men on the floor. He rolled up the dead man's sleeve and saw what he expected to find. Reese pushed the door open and ran to Thomas giving him a hug, then asked what he was looking at. Thomas looked down at the tattoo again.

"Grimes was right, the Russians are involved. That tattoo," Thomas explained. "Is a Spetsnaz tattoo."

Chapter 23.

August 3$^{rd.}$, Detroit, Michigan.

It was pouring rain as Isaack walked across the truck stop parking lot. He was walking towards a black Suburban that was parked at the back of the lot between a couple tractor truck trailers out of sight. He opened the back-passenger side door and stepped inside out of the rain. Boris and Costner sat in the front looking back at him. Boris in his deep accent said, "Greetings, my friend." Isaack greeted both men back then asked,

"We agreed no more meetings, what is going on?" directing the question at Boris, who was in the passenger seat in front of him. Boris continued looking forward and stated coldly,

"Grimes is dead, and there was an attempt on Shura." Costner became angry and shouted at Boris,

"I thought you had people watching Grimes!" Coldly Boris replied to Costner,

"I did, that is why he is dead!" Costner rolled his head back in frustration and asked,

"Did you kill him?"

"Yes, well my men did, but then someone killed my men." Boris vaguely explained while Isaack sat quietly in the back listening. Costner was frustrated, and was demanding answers,

"You said someone made an attempt on Shura's life? I am sure someone did, she is an arms dealer. How do you know it was not a rival dealer, which I am sure happens all the time? Why are you

189

insinuating it had something to do with our business?" Costner asked impatiently. Boris looked at him and said softly,

"These men were very professional. Much too good for thugs, I believe it was these men who took out the weapons shipments in Turkey and Morocco." Costner grabbed the wheel turning his body at Boris and shouted, "You said that was the Brits or the French!"
"I do not think that anymore," Boris replied calmly. Isaack, who had been silent until now asked,
"Boris, get on with it. Why are we here, and why did you kill Grimes?" Boris readjusted himself in the seat to see Isaack in the backseat.
"My men were living across the road from Grimes. They would take pictures of everyone going in and out of Grimes' home. Then they would run them on the facial recognition computer on the spot. Well a few days ago, Grimes got visitors from America, one was a very beautiful FBI agent named Reese Gilbert and the other, a Thomas Price, a known operative for a private military company called Capital Intel Group. This company is known to do much work for the CIA," Boris explained, looking at Costner almost accusingly. Costner immediately got defensive,

"Listen Boris, we have people in both CIA and FBI headquarters, and they are not doing any investigating on our activities." Boris then handed a folder to Costner, who took it and opened it. Then Boris sarcastically said,

"Yes, but do you have a person in the Capital Intel Group?" In the folder, there was several pictures of Reese and Thomas entering Grimes' house. As he flipped through the pictures there was more pictures of both from government identifications to their friend's social media sites. There was even a picture of Thomas and his entire Ranger unit taken in the field while he was deployed in Afghanistan, and one from Iraq as well. Costner finished then handed the folder back to Isaack as Boris the went on explaining,

"The two operatives entered Grimes' office while my men ran their faces, it was noticed they were in there a long time. My people had a hack on Grimes' personal computer, as well as his network server in his house, and found he was accessing files directly involving our activities. They contacted me, and I gave the kill order for all three."

"So, they are all dead then?" Isaack asked.

"No, this Thomas Price killed my men. Grimes is dead, but the FBI women and Price are still alive, and they took Grimes' computer. I fear Grimes has placed the entire operation in jeopardy." The three men sat silent until Costner spoke.

"Grimes may have had information on the accounts, but the FBI would need names and places here in the United States to stop anything, and I doubt Grimes would have that in his computer. I mean, we purposely kept him in the dark." Boris nodded his head in agreement.

191

Isaack opened the folder with the pictures as he began looking through it and said,

"Sounds like this Price guys is someone I need with me, if he killed four of your men himself." He kept looking through he pictures until he came to a unit photo of Price's Ranger unit and at that moment he went into a state of shock and then froze. He was looking at Thomas Price alright, but the man beside him with his arm leaning on Thomas' shoulder was Paul Totten. The young man he had placed so much trust in, and who had witnessed him murder a man. Isaack began talking fast,

"The mission is in jeopardy, real jeopardy!" He explained what he had seen in the photo and everyone knew it was not a coincidence. "I have to go home and prepare for the attack, we are doing it as soon as possible, and when I mean as soon as possible, I mean in the next several days. I will send every person I have into hiding immediately. We have already arranged everything and have our staging areas picked out in DC ready and waiting for us. Costner texts me daily reports of the President's locations. It is time," Isaack stated as he opened the door and stepped out in the rain. Costner asked,

"How will we know when the attack is coming?"

"If I am unable to contact you, you will know when the shooting starts," Isaack said and quickly walked away.

Chapter 24.

August 3rd. Flint, Michigan.

Paul was at the MLB compound's shooting range working Kelly Alderman trying to teach her how to shoot at long distances, not that Paul ever claimed he was an expert himself at long distances. Since his time with the MLB, he and Kelly had become quite close over the past several months and she would confide in him often of her home life, living with an abusive husband. Paul promised himself when this over he was going to pay her husband a visit with a baseball bat.

"Okay listen, now control your breathing like I showed you," Paul explained to Kelly as she took aim at a target four hundred yards out and squeezed the trigger, but nothing happened. "Kelly, load the weapon," Paul said, laughing at her,

"Shut up! Jackass." Kelly said, laughing with him. Paul was dressed in the MLB uniform and had his Glock 9mm loaded and holstered on his side. As Kelly was loading the rifle, Paul heard an engine coming up behind him. He turned to see Isaack's 2017 black Chevy Silverado parking. Isaack, Alfred and two of Alfred's asshole friends stepped out and began walking towards them. Paul waved at Isaack and continued his instruction with Kelly. She took her time and pulled the trigger. Paul held up his spotting scope and looked at the target, "Nice shot," he said happily to Kelly who was looking at him, but not smiling. Paul instantly knew something was wrong and turned around to see Isaack holding a Smith and Wesson M&P 45 at his head. Alfred walked up and removed Paul's Glock from his holster, then said smiling at Paul,

"I said from day one you were a pig." Paul never had time to let the fear set in before someone hit him in the back of the head.

Paul did not know how long it was before he woke up covered in horse shit, tied up in one of the horse barns. The back of his head was aching, blood had run down the back of his head and neck. He was naked with not a stitch of clothing on, and he was handcuffed to a chain that was hooked to an electric pulley lift, attached to the ceiling some twelve feet above him. Paul knew there was only one reason he would be in this really serious predicament, and that would be because Isaack had found out why he was there. "Well, I am completely fucked!" Paul said aloud. Just then Alfred came walking in with Isaack and two friends,

"Well, well, well." Alfred said smiling like he was going to have way too much fun this day. Isaack walked over to the lift controls pressing the button and raising the chain and Paul's hands with it, until it lifted Paul off the ground several inches. The handcuffs dug into the bones in Paul's wrists causing him terrific pain. Alfred then walked over in front of Paul. He was holding a roll of duct tape in his hands. Laughing, he walked around behind Paul and knelt and taped his feet together.

"Now, I know you know how to use those feet, so let me take care of them." Alfred said as he broke off the roll and tossed it to one of his friends.

Paul's wrists were aching from the handcuffs already, even before Alfred started punching him in the stomach, violently pushing all the air from his lungs out of his body. Alfred was taking special delight in this, and it showed as he grinned so hard all his teeth were visible. Isaack lowered the lift down allowing Paul to hold his own weight, but his arms were still suspended over his head.

Isaack slowly walked over in front of Paul smoking his cigarette,

"Paul, I just want you to know you are going to die, whether it is in five minutes or in five days is up to you. We need some answers before we let you rest in peace." Isaack then held up the picture of Thomas and Paul together with their old unit, and asked Paul if he knew him. Paul knew there was no reason to lie, they already knew Paul had a friendship with Thomas or he would not be in this spot, besides he was standing beside the man in the picture.

"Yes, I know him." Paul answered, still trying to catch his breath.

"Good Paul, we are building trust," Isaack said arrogantly while pulling out a second picture of Reese taken while she sat in a car in Zurich with Thomas and held it up to Paul's face.

Paul looked at her and wished he was with her now. Her soft skin, beautiful smile and hypnotic eyes.

"No," Paul answered. Isaack put the picture back into the folder, then took a drag off the cigarette making sure he had the end nice and hot and then pressed it into Paul's chest. Paul jerked back away from the burn and Isaack then stepped away, lighting another smoke. Then he sat down on a bale of hay and began the interrogation,

"Who do you work for?" Isaack asked as Alfred and his friends surrounded Paul. Paul said nothing. He was not about to put Thomas and Reese in any jeopardy, they were his true best friends. "This woman Reese the FBI lady, what did you tell her?" Isaack asked.

Paul refused to say anything. Isaack nodded at Alfred who was standing behind Paul and placed a black plastic bag over Paul's head and tightened it around his neck cutting off Paul's air as he held it tight. Paul held his breath for as long as he could, his lungs began burning and still he held his breath. Soon he needed air and tried to breath in but he could get nothing. He exhaled all he had in his lungs then sucked it back in finding little relief. In another few seconds he began thrashing, trying to break Alfred's seal on the bag, but nothing he did helped and panic set in. Paul even tried crying out and felt himself getting light headed. He heard Isaack's voice say something and Alfred removed the bag. Paul gasped for air, the life giving sweet

196

air, his heart was racing, his lungs were burning, and his head was spinning. Paul thought to himself that was even worse than when they water boarded him in Fort Benning during his interrogation training which he thought had sucked at the time.

Isaack began asking more questions, Paul still refused to answer so, he received the bag once more. Isaack asked again, and Paul was given the bag again, but still he refused to talk. Paul felt content to die this night, he always had the ability to take punishment, and drive his body through the pain. He did it with football, and in the military. He tried placing his mind into somewhere he felt safe and happy, and ended up in Reese's bed. He was happily holding her naked body tight to his own… Until Alfred placed the bag over his head again and screwed that moment up, but before Alfred sealed the bag around his neck, Paul exhaled all his air. Maybe, he thought, he could help end this faster, and it did not take long before he lost consciousness.

Paul awoke an unknown amount of time later. He was lying on his back on the floor of the barn in the horse shit. Kelly stood over him looking down at him. She was visibly upset, and had been crying,

"You broke my heart, Paul," she shouted sobbing, and Isaack pressed the button raising Paul upright again. Paul looked into her eyes. He could see her pain, not for him but for the loss of her son and living with her abusive husband. Paul actually found shame inside himself for betraying Kelly. He dropped his head and quietly said to her,

"I am sorry." Kelly looked at him and began weeping, then slapped him across the face hard and walked out of the barn looking at Isaack and said,

"Kill him!" as she left the barn.

"Well, the bag didn't work," Isaack said, standing up and walking over to Paul. "You are tough Paul, I respect that about you. But I must go. Because of you and your friends, we are going into hiding. Alfred here is going to stay with you for a while and see what he can get you to say. It was nice knowing you Paul," Isaack stated and took Alfred away and had a talk out of earshot from Paul, then he left taking one of Alfred's friends with him.

Alfred walked over to a small room off the front of the barn and came back with a red and white three-foot-long electric cattle prod, and an electric branding iron. He plugged the iron into the wall and Paul watched it getting hot fast. Alfred was smiling like an idiot as he walked over to Paul and touched the prod to Paul's back. Paul jumped and jerked as the prod shocked him. "Fuck!" Paul shouted as Alfred hit him repeatedly sending an intense shock through his body. Alfred was laughing hysterically, and Paul knew his remaining hours would be more of the same until his heart gave out.

"Alfred!" Paul shouted, Alfred stopped and looked at him, Paul began taunting him, "You are such a pussy, you and your fucking retarded group of friends who think you're tough, but you're not. You can't fight, and you know it." Alfred walked up to Paul and struck him in the face hard. Paul 's nose began to bleed, but he did not think it was broken. "You see Alfred, you proved my point. You are afraid, that is why you only challenged me after you were drunk and now I am tied up."

"SHUT UP!" Alfred screamed at Paul and punched him again in the stomach, taking his wind again, it was almost a minute before Paul was able to talk again. He could see Alfred was raging.

"Come on Alfred, admit it. You're fucking scared, that is why you hit the gym so hard, that is why you inject the juice into your ass." Alfred was raging and was pacing back and forth and just kept saying,

"No way man, no way!" Paul looked at Alfred's friend who stood watching not saying anything,

"Hey, tell me, have you ever seen him fight someone he might have had a slim chance of losing the fight too?" Alfred's friend stood thinking, then got a mild look of confusion on his face and looked at Alfred. Realizing his friend may be silently agreeing with Paul, Alfred began yelling at his friend, threatening to assault him.

Paul knew he had a shot, a slim one, but a shot, "Alfred, I bet you won't try me out," Paul shouted. Alfred left his friend and walked to Paul.

"What did you say?" Alfred asked clenching his teeth. "I am going to die, but before you shoot me in the head, try me out. Last time you were drunk, you're not now. You have worked me over all night here. I am not ready for this, so try me out," Paul whispered, making sure his friend would not hear it.

Alfred stepped back from Paul almost shaking. Paul knew he only would have to push him a little more. "Come on you pussy! Are the steroids taking your manhood from you?" Paul shouted, and Alfred screamed in rage,

"Fuck you!" at Paul and turned to his friend telling him to cut Paul down. The two had an argument, then finally the friend gave up. He walked over and hit the button letting Paul's hands down and then cutting his feet lose. Finally, he took off the handcuffs and Paul rubbed his wrists. The relief he felt from the removal of the handcuffs was incredible, but he felt weak.

"Can I have some clothes? You don't want to do this with me naked, do you?" Paul asked, and the friend walked over to the other side of the barn where Paul's clothes were piled and tossed him his boxers. Alfred took off his gun belt and handed it to his friend, then peeled off his shirt and began flexing like the Hulk. Paul shook his head at the ridiculous show, and knew he had to figure something out soon, because the friend held his pistol out on Paul covering him the entire time.

Alfred looked at his friend and said,

"If I lose this fight, just shoot him dead!" Then he charged at Paul.

The charging bull came across the barn at Paul full out. Paul managed to push off his body and get out of the way. As Alfred ran past him Paul stepped in closer to him and before Alfred could turn around, Paul kicked Alfred on the thigh as hard as he could, then quickly stepped away. Paul knew the only way he could win this fight was to not let the steroid raging maniac get a hold of him. He had plenty of room in the barn to move around and thought he better use it and began moving away. Alfred rubbed his leg and came at Paul again. Paul backed away and when Alfred came closer to swing at him, Paul kicked him in the thigh again, hard, and Alfred stumbled as his thigh muscle seemed to tighten up on him.

Back at Fort Benning Paul would train often at night in the base gym in martial arts and he loved the sparring. Paul had an instructor who taught them to kick the legs on bigger opponents to slow them down. Paul knew that this was the time to put that lesson into practice.

Alfred started following Paul as he backed away and began to circle. Paul would slow down just enough for Alfred to come in close and then he would kick his right thigh as hard as he could, then back away. After the fifth or sixth kick Alfred was in pain and began to get frustrated and charged at Paul again arms open like he was going to pick up a barrel and crush it. This left his body wide open and Paul threw a hard-right hand striking the bull in the face and breaking his nose.

Alfred fell to the ground, Paul stepped behind him and wrapped his arms around his neck in the sleeper hold trying to make Alfred fall asleep. The strong young man grabbed Paul's arms and pulled down hard and they fell to the dirty floor rolling around. Paul was losing his grip, his arms felt weak from the night of abuse he had been dealt and Alfred was just too strong.

As they rolled on the floor in the horse shit and straw, Paul noticed they were getting closer to the electric branding iron that Alfred had plugged in some time ago, and it was damn hot now as it glowed red hot. The friend that was to be covering Paul with a gun was really enjoying the fight, and moved over closer to see if Alfred was going to pass out. He started cheering his friend on, "Come buddy, break his grip!" he yelled to Alfred. Paul used everything he had to move Alfred closer to the wall and the friend came in a little closer. In a blink, Paul let go of Alfred and reached for the iron taking hold of the handle, then rolled his body towards the unsuspecting guard and pressed the hot end into his face. The young friend screamed as one of his eyes was hit by the iron and instantly rendered the eye useless on the spot, and deep burns covered the left side his face. Paul hit him again with the iron a second time, as the friend tried pushing the red-hot iron away with his hands, causing him to drop his Ruger SR9 9mm pistol to the ground. Paul then struck the young man in the head with the handle of the iron and reached for the Ruger, but was tackled by Alfred, and they both fell to the ground.

Paul was rolled to his back and Alfred wrapped his hand around Paul's throat and began squeezing hard trying to take the life out of Paul. Paul did not have the strength to fight off Alfred, he began reaching around trying to find something to use against Alfred before he went unconscious but could find nothing. In one final attempt to save his life, Paul brought his hand up between Alfred's arms and using it like lever he pried one of Alfred's hands loose making his body drop just enough for Paul to thrust his finger deep into Alfred's right eye. Instinctively Alfred leaned his body back, and Paul thrust his fist up and struck Alfred in the throat causing him to fall backwards.

Paul rolled over, and crawled to the Ruger, reached for it and as soon as he felt it in his hand he racked the slide then rolled to his back again. Alfred was on his feet now and coming for Paul screaming. Paul used his thumb and switched the safety off and pulled the trigger. The Ruger bucked in his hand and the round hit Alfred in the throat, causing him to drop on the ground with both hands on his throat. The half blind friend realized what was happening, he desperately reached for Paul, but it was in vain when the muzzle of his own pistol pressed against his good eye and the trigger was pulled.

Paul then stood up and walked over to Alfred. He looked down at him as he squirmed on the ground holding his throat and blood was pouring out over his hands.

"Help me," Alfred pleaded to Paul as blood bubbled out of his mouth.

"God, you're so fucking stupid!" Paul replied coldly and shot Alfred in the face.

Chapter 25.

August 2nd. Flint, Michigan.

Paul sat in the barn for some time, he was trying to let his body recover from the hours he was chained up and tortured. He had found a water tap and drank the cold refreshing water, which helped some. He washed himself as clean as he could, then went and donned his clothes. He even found his belt and gun and placed it on. He needed to eat, his body was craving food, mostly sugar. He took the Ruger he had killed Alfred and his friend with along with all the ammo he could find on their bodies.

After an about an hour he was confident now he was as good as he was going to get until he could find some food and made his way to the door of the barn and slowly opened it. "Thank god, it is dark," he silently whispered to himself and moved outside slowly and looked around getting his bearings. He was in the center of the compound close to Isaack's house and the trailer park. Paul knew he had to be careful, the compound was covered in cameras and thankfully he had been studying the placement and fields of vision ever since he first was allowed inside.

He kept low as he moved into the trees and began heading to where he thought he may be able to find a rifle and maybe a vehicle. As he made his way towards the trailer park his ribs were reminding him of Alfred fists with every step. As he was passing the vehicle park that had all the school buses and tractor trucks and trailers, Winnebago's, etc., he instantly noticed they were all gone, all of them. Paul thought Isaack must have moved them out to go into hiding like he said, or maybe he was starting his operation, the ACT as Isaack had called it. Paul knew he needed to call Reese or Thomas, or simply the goddamn cops, but first he needed a phone. He continued his way to the trailer park hoping not to run into anyone. Usually he would hear noises by now like a vehicle or people walking, maybe the kids playing, but the compound was quiet. He crawled closer using the tall grass outside of the trees near the trailer park, it seemed deserted but there were some lights left on.

Paul stood and casually walked in, he was still wearing the MLB uniform, he even kept the beret on as he walked to the first trailer and checked the door, it was not locked, and he walked in. No one was home, so he went to the fridge and grabbed an apple and started eating. There was a chocolate bar in the door, and he ate that too as fast as he could. He took some juice boxes and drank them as he went to the washroom and had a movement. Then searched the house for weapons, which was not hard to find. In the bedroom in the closet there were at least eight rifles being stored.
The weapon he chose was a Ruger SR-762 AR-10, because it had four loaded twenty round magazines containing the .308 ammo required for it. The weapon had no after market optics, just the

206

iron sites, but Paul did not mind. He just felt better having something in his hands that he could reach out and touch someone with. He placed one mag in the rifle and the other three in his pants pockets, then returned to the fridge for more food. Grabbing some ham and a bun off the table he ate them both quickly, washing it down with more juice.

Paul went over the place looking for a phone, or a computer with Internet access but had no luck. He realized that his only way of getting word out was to get himself out of the compound. He left the trailer and began making his way to the outer fence. Paul then heard voices, and to his surprise there were people still here. Paul laid down in the grass listening, it was a woman's voice with children inside one of the trailers. Once he deemed it safe, he began moving again.

After several minutes of crawling he had made it in sight of the outer fence, and he could see all the guard towers were manned. There was also a mobile patrol in a pick-up truck driving the perimeter with an armed man riding in the back. The fence was lit up with bright lights. Paul realized cutting through the fence was out and retreated into the bushes. Sooner or later he knew someone would find out he had escaped the barn and they would begin looking for him, so he had to find a way out soon. Paul thought of how inmates in prison must feel when they think about escape, towers, fences, and guards, same thing he thought, then wondered why he was sympathizing with criminals, he never gave a shit about criminals.

He decided to make his way to the main gate. Maybe he could find a vehicle there and crash the fence. It took him an hour to make his way unseen to the front gate. Hiding in the trees Paul stood back watching and counting. He could see six men, not including the closest tower guard, so that made seven. One in the gatehouse, two outside talking, one working on a pickup trying unsuccessfully to get it running, two more walking as if they were on a patrol, plus the tower and the two in the truck patrolling the perimeter. Paul knew he was good but, "Shit," he whispered. At his best taking out this many armed men would be a stretch, but after the night he had he thought it was impossible. He studied the situation and realized his best route would be to walk out the front door and maybe take out some men quiet like on his way.

He sat silent watching and counting times and patterns and decided now his best chance was to wait for when the two guys walking were at their farthest point from the gatehouse. He stood up and casually walked to the gate house hoping they would not recognize him in the darkness, plus he still had on his uniform. He walked to the truck the one guy was working on, casually and silently walked up behind him. From that point the man was close enough to the gatehouse that neither the tower guard or anyone else was able to see him. The truck he was working on blocked any view of the two men just hanging around talking. Paul walked up and pulled his knife off his belt, taking the man with his left hand cupping his mouth and silently drove his knife into the base of his skull into his brain.

Paul gently lay the man's body down on the ground and took a fast look around. No one had seen anything. He quickly wiped the blood off his knife, then began walking to the gatehouse door. As he reached for the door handle one of the two men talking saw him and called out to him. Paul acted like he never heard them and entered the building closing the door behind him. The man inside the gate house looked at Paul as he tried to hide his face from the guard. The guard recognized him immediately, and without saying a word the guard went for his side arm. Ready for this, Paul lifted his rifle to his shoulder and let one round loose. The large .308 round made half the man's head cover the wall behind him and his body fell to the floor. The two guards outside that had called out to him burst through the back door to find Paul waiting for them. Paul was kneeling behind counter with the rifle at his shoulder pointed at the door. He killed them both with two quick shots to the chest each.

The gatehouse door only needed to be buzzed opened from the outside, on the inside all you needed to do was push on the lever and it would pop open. Paul pressed the lever, opened the door and ran out, but remembered the tower guard had a perfect view of the parking lot. Paul turned his body around and walked backwards holding his rifle to his shoulder moving away from the gatehouse. He kept walking backwards until he got far away from the gatehouse and he had a line of sight to the tower that covered the area. Paul saw the top of the tower guard's head before he saw him, and he shot the tower guard before the man had even seen him exit the building.

He then turned and ran to his pickup that was still sitting in the parking lot which he had left the keys in. The two guards who had been on foot patrol opened fire on him through the fence. Paul's line of sight with them was broken by several vehicles in the parking lot, as he had always parked in the back of the lot.

Paul could hear the engine of the mobile patrol coming towards him and jumped into his pickup, started it and began speeding away from the compound, he looked into the rear-view mirror and could see the patrol truck coming after him. He pushed the gas pedal to the floor wanting to get as far away from the compound as he could before he dealt with these two behind him.

Once he hit the main road he stopped the truck and jumped out, placing a fresh twenty round magazine into the rifle and laid his body flat on the highway, facing down the laneway to the compound. He took another mag out his pocket and lay it down beside him and got ready. He waited for the truck to get about one hundred yards away before he started shooting. He began firing at a rate of two rounds per second. The man standing in the box started shooting back, but Paul took closer aim and hit him in the chest and he dropped down into the box. The driver slammed on the breaks and stopped, it was clear he was panicking as he climbed out jumping into the ditch for cover. Paul reloaded his rifle and fired five rounds into the tall grass keeping the man's head down. Then he stood, firing five more as he slowly walked back to his truck, five more before climbing inside, then he closed the door and put it in gear and sped off.

He drove fast gaining distance, he decided not to head into Flint, instead he went east. He drove flat out for about twenty minutes and once he knew he was away from the compound and not being followed, he pulled over and stopped. He reached into the glove box removing his wallet and cell phone, he stepped out of the truck onto the road into the darkness. He took off his belt and holster then tossed it in the truck, threw the beret and tiger stripped shirt into the ditch leaving the pants and woodland green t-shirt on.

Paul took his phone and was about to call Reese's number, but he found himself getting upset. He knew it was the adrenaline and tried calming himself. He then called Reese's number and let it ring, she did not answer, it went to voice mail and he hung up. Frustrated, he called Thomas' cell and it rang, and went to voice mail. Paul was feeling emotional, it had been one hell of a bad night and was approaching two am. His emotions and anxiety were beginning to take over, he felt like he was going to lose control,

"Fuck! Ranger up Paul!" He shouted and knew if he went to Flint they would be looking for him there and he was not even sure if Reese would be there or not. He had not heard from her since she said they were looking into the money. He tried her number again and it went to voicemail.

The emotions and anxiety were still building, and he felt so alone at this moment, he tried Thomas' number again and it to went to voicemail, Paul waited for the prompt him to talk, "Where the fuck are you!" he shouted into the phone and hung it up. He tossed the phone onto the seat of the truck and began pacing on the road hands on his hips. "Calm down buddy!" Paul said aloud to himself trying keep his composure, but it was too late. He lost it and began punching the box of his truck screaming out loud into the darkness as he continued punching repeatedly in frustration.

He had the worst feeling that Isaack had Reese, he was scared they may be doing to her what was done to him this night. He needed to know if she and Thomas were safe, but had no place to start. All Paul could think about was killing Isaack and wished he had done it weeks ago. He climbed back into the truck and started driving east. If he hurried, he could be at CIG headquarters in about eight hours and that was the only thing he could think of. He became overly worried that they had Reese and had began thinking of going back to the compound to make someone talk, but decided against it as he knew he needed to find help.

He had been driving for less than a minute when his phone rang. The sound of the ringer made him jump in his seat, he grabbed the phone while slamming on the brakes and pulling over. He looked at the phone and it was showing an unknown number, he answered the phone,

"Hello!"

"Hello Paul Totten." Paul jumped as he heard Isaack's voice on the other end, rage and adrenaline filled Paul's body.

"What do you want Isaack, is this where you threaten me?" Paul asked as his hands shook.

"I just want to let you know you are too late. Everything is in place!" Isaack so calmly informed him. Paul's stomach began turning.

"You're a fucking lunatic!" Paul yelled into the phone, then Paul heard Isaack laughing as the phone went dead. Paul set the phone down on the seat and cursed aloud again.

Suddenly the phone rang again, Paul picked it up and seen Reese's name on the screen. He answered it. "Reese." Paul yelled and began weeping at the sound of her voice. Concern came to her voice as she heard his emotion.

"Are you okay?" she asked him.

"I don't know, I am now, I guess" he said as he struggled with his emotions.

"Paul, you are on speaker phone in the CIG board room. Everyone that was here last time you were here is present, do you recall?" Reese asked him, trying to be as discreet as possible in case someone was listening. Paul understood immediately what she was talking about and that she was in a meeting with Directors, Bryant and Cromwell. It felt so good to hear her voice, Paul held back more tears. "Paul, what is wrong?" Reese asked,

"Oh, well, you know Isaack found out about me then they knocked me out, I got tortured, killed about ten guys escaping the fucking compound! A fucking lunatic is phoning me taunting me, and not one of you guys will answer your GOD DAMN PHONES!" Paul screamed, "Oh, and did I mention they fucking tortured me!" Paul continued yelling. Paul could hear a conversation in the boardroom and recognized Bryant's voice who then spoke directly to Paul,

"Paul drive to the nearest airport, we are sending the CIG plane to pick you up and bring you here. We cannot talk about this on a cell phone. Do you understand?"

"Yes sir, I do. Send a plane to the Ann Arbor airport. I will meet it there." Paul said regaining his composure and hung up the phone. "This fucking sucks!" Paul said aloud to himself as he started driving again.

Chapter 26.

Aug 4th. Davidsonville, Maryland. Capital Intel Group facility.

Paul had met the plane at the Ann Arbor municipal airport, and as soon a Paul got aboard it immediately returned to the air. Thomas and Tim O'Brien were both armed and waiting on board for him with a CIG combat medic. The sight of his two buddies helped bring him down from the dark place he was in before he entered the plane. After checking his vitals, the medic opened the mini bar and prescribed a triple bourbon to calm him down.

The flight was fast, it was now less than seven hours since Paul had contacted Reese and they applauded him as he walked into the boardroom. He still had on his tiger striped camo pants and woodland green t-shirt. He was also wearing his belt and holster with his loaded Glock. Thomas knew better than to try and take it from him with his current state of mind. The boardroom had the same people in it as it did the last time Paul had been here when they recruited him for this mission, except this time breakfast sandwiches and hot coffee were provided.

Paul began briefing everyone in the room of the events from the past several days. When Paul got to the escape portion of his briefing he was not sure if he killed seven guys or eight while escaping, "or was it nine?" Paul said, then paused as he was thinking. Director Cromwell looked at Director Bryant and smiled, which was returned with the

215

middle figure. He told them that Isaack had said they were going into hiding and disappointed them when he could not say where, and they were even more disappointed when he had no new information on Martin Sibley for them. They then began talking of a plan of action now. They all knew it was time to talk to President Hunton. Paul was on his third breakfast sandwich when Reese poured him a cup of hot coffee, as he listened to the two directors talking about their course of action. Paul stood up and walked over to the window with his coffee and looked out. He was finally starting to relax after the past day. Looking out the window he saw Tim and his team working in the kill house again and for the first time Paul had zero desire to go play with them. He was spent and all he wanted to do was to climb into bed with Reese and sleep for a week.

He stood sipping the hot coffee listening to Cromwell and Bryant talking strategy of how to deliver this to the President. Reese again asked to take Paul to the hospital for an examination. His face was swollen, and his abdomen looked like he was hit by a truck. She had commented more than once, and Paul simply replied, "I am fine."

Bryant picked up the phone and called his office asking his secretary to set up an emergency meeting with the President as soon as possible, then hung up the phone. Then Bryant walked over to Paul holding his hand out in front of him and said,

"Well done son, be proud of what you have done here." Paul shook the man's hand not saying anything, he just smiled. A few people in the room applauded him again when a gunshot was heard coming from outside. Everyone in the room stopped what they were doing and looked at each other in confusion. Thomas lifted his hands up and said,

"Don't worry, the boys are working the kill house again this morning. Tim likes to keep them sharp." Everyone began talking again when another gunshot was heard, this time louder and it sounded like it came from the opposite direction than of the kill house to the front of the facility, not the back where the kill house was located. Thomas jumped up running for the boardroom door looking down the hallway when the gunfire then sounded from inside the CIG headquarters building itself. Paul ran to the door with Thomas and yelled,

"Holy shit! It's Isaack's people!" as he pulled out his Glock from its holster. Reese made her way beside him with her Sig in her hand. Paul looked at her holding her sidearm. They were the only two that were armed. Thomas looked at them both, then at his empty hands and shouted to Paul,

"We have a sweet armoury here, if we can get to it." Paul looked at Thomas agreeing with him and said,

"Yes, let's go man!" He called for everyone to follow them. As they left the boardroom heading down the hallway and descended the stairwell, some CIG office employees ran up the stairs past them in full panic mode. Paul was the first one to hit the ground floor and he moved into the lobby with his Glock held at eye level. He saw a masked man in tiger striped camo who was spraying the offices with an AK-47 while laughing, his bullets easily passed through the drywall walls of several offices. Paul quickly took aim and shot the man in the head; his body instantly fell limp to the floor. Thomas immediately ran to him retrieving his weapons and tac vest, then tossed the man's side arm to Director Bryant and then began to move again as he placed a fresh mag inside the weapon. An explosion rocked the front of the building as someone had shot a vehicle that was trying to leave the lot with an RPG blowing out all the windows in the front of the building.

"GO, GO, GO!" Thomas yelled to everyone after the glass stopped flying all over the lobby and led them to the back of the building and outside. They entered the storage area for the shop where the vehicles were being armoured up in. Several trucks and vans were sitting out there and made good cover as they slowly moved their way to the team's combat preparation and training building. Thomas yelled for everyone to get down as a rocket hit the side of the headquarters building and exploded. Then an intensive amount of rifle and machine gun fire began tearing up everything around them. Everyone ran behind an armoured vehicle, they were unable to move in any direction. Thomas moved to the corner of the vehicle he was taking cover behind and began returning fire and Paul did the same from another vehicle. Paul looked out at the attackers and there was more than he was expecting to see. He counted at least twenty.

"This is bad!" Paul shouted to Thomas who looked at him smiling and shouted back,

"Hey at least we found the smuggled weapons. They are using them to kill us," and both men laughed. Paul seen a short attacker moving to his left trying to take a flanking position on them. The attacker moved behind a scrap metal bin for cover. Paul knew he could not let that person get any farther to his left or they would be in real trouble. He held the Glock in both hands aiming at the top of the bin and waited for this person to either jump up or move positions. One second later the attacker made a break going farther on the flank. Paul snapped off two rounds with both hitting the masked attacker in the torso and dropped him. Paul broke cover and ran to the man he had just shot to retrieve the weapons. Once he got there and began relieving the weapons and ammo from his body, he noticed the person was still alive. He reached down and lifted the mask, and Paul was horrified to see that he had just shot Kelly Alderman.

He pulled her over to cover and tried holding her hand, she was choking on blood and with her last bit of strength she tried punching Paul's face. Her arms dropped to her side and she quit breathing. Without another thought, Paul dropped the magazine of the AK-47 and placed in a new one. He moved to his left and found a good position and opened fire towards the attackers who were trying to advance on them. The sound of gunfire suddenly doubled, then Paul realized the new gunshots were not the common sounds of the traditional Kalashnikov. It was the sound newer western built rifles made when being fired.

Tim and his team had moved into position and were now advancing on the attackers aggressively, killing them as they moved. Once the CIG combatants came into this fight the tables had turned and it was hardly a fair fight for the MLB at all. It was evident that the MLB fighters came here thinking they were going to kill some office staff or maybe an over educated lawyer or two, not finding one of the world's most elite and already geared up and armed special ops units. The remaining MLB began to run trying to save themselves but, were cut down quickly. Tim yelled for his men to sweep every building, then sweep them again.

"Bring me one alive if you can!" He shouted as he walked over to Paul. "I see your friends showed up, what the hell did they come here for?" Tim asked Paul, but before he could answer Tim added, "These guys were chumps, man!"

Paul left Tim and ran over to Reese making sure she was okay. She was sitting on the ground looking at a hole in the leg of her pantsuit and when she saw Paul coming she stood and ran to him giving him a big hug.

"How do you guys always stay so calm through this shit?" she asked as she buried her face in his chest. Paul never said anything and just held her and turned his gaze over to Kelly's body, and reminded himself that her husband still needed that ass kicking.

Bryant got on the phone and called the FBI headquarters informing them of what had gone down.

"I want a full team here now!" Bryant ordered on the phone, then hung it up. He then pointed at Tim and shouted,

"You, secure the area! NOW!" Paul heard Bryant yell to Tim and smiled because he knew what would be coming back from Tim. Tim walked up to Bryant, taking his trigger finger and poked him in the chest and shouted back,

"Listen, fuck face! I don't know who you are and I don't care, but securing the area is kind of basic standard and is already being done now by my guys! Second, don't talk to me like that! We just saved your ass! Why the fuck don't you go back inside and grab me a coffee! Two sugars!" Bryant stood in a state of shock unable to speak as Tim walked away changing the mag in his rifle and muttering something to himself. Reese having watched the entire thing still holding Paul tightly and said,

"I thought Canadians were supposed to be nice."

Chapter 27.

Aug 4th. Washington D.C. Arlington National Cemetery.

President Sterling Hunton stood over his father's grave with his son Marty at Arlington National Cemetery. Sterling's father had been a Marine who had died in Vietnam on this date in 1971. Sterling and his son made the pilgrimage here to pay their respects to him every year or as much as possible.

"I wish I'd known him," Marty said to his father as he placed a small flag in the ground beside his headstone. Sterling looked proudly at his son, who for this occasion wore his dress blues. Marty D. Sterling was twenty-six years old and was a proud member of the United States Marines and took his duties as a lieutenant seriously. He could have used his father's connections and taken an easy route but always chose the hard, proud road, just like his father had. He had been training his body hard for the Forced Recon tryouts, which he wanted badly. His father commented on how much muscle he had put on recently and that he had chosen to shave his head bald these days.

Almost every male of the Sterling family had spent time in the Marines. It was more than a family tradition, it was a calling for them. Marty had served a tour in Afghanistan where he was wounded, and many said this helped his father win the election. Marty joked with his father, "I took the golden bullet for you, Dad."

"Your grandfather would have loved you," Sterling said to his son and became emotional.

"Dad the cameras," Marty said to his father as he stepped in front of him to block the cameras, "Who says a man cannot shed a tear at his father's grave," and gently he pushed him aside not caring who saw him.

The Secret Service agents looked outwards in all directions keeping a close eye on everyone and everything and their motorcade was nearby ready to move on a moment's notice.

"I forgot to ask. Where is mom?" Marty asked his father. Sterling wiped the final tear off his face and smiled at his son,

"She is in New York today for one of her charities, some ladies luncheon," he said smiling.

One of President Sterling's aides came walking up, "Sorry sir, we have had numerous calls from Director Bryant and Director Cromwell both asking for a sit-down meeting. Both are saying it is an emergency and it is for your ears only." Sterling looked at the aide wondering what could be so important that both FBI and CIA directors need a sit-down

"Okay." The President replied, "Tell them I will be leaving for my office right away and to meet me there, please make the arrangements." Sterling said politely, then placed his hand on his fathers gravestone. "See you later dad." Sterling said and began walking away with his son.

The father and son walked side by side to the presidential limousine and climbed in. The Secret Service agents ran for their designated vehicles and climbed in and the motorcade began moving.

"I like riding in this, I bet if I was riding in this in Afghanistan I would not have gotten hit, and the AC is way better." Marty joked to his father who laughed.

"How you fixed for money? Do you need any?" Sterling asked his son, who started laughing.

"Dad I am earning money, and I am twenty-six, not sixteen. I am fine." They smiled at each other as the twelve-vehicle motorcade had began moving as several marked police cars left ahead of him to block traffic, allowing a fast commute back the White House which was only a few miles away. They entered the Arlington National bridge moving back across the Potomac River when the limo started slowing down. Sterling noticed the escorting vehicles began tightening up around the limo, so tight they blocked all vision outside. Suddenly a large explosion was heard in front of them, followed by some intensive gunfire. The motorcade was stopped by another large explosion. The Secret Service were shouting on the radio and the driver slammed the large limo in reverse and gunned it. The powerful engine whined as it accelerated the heavy vehicle backwards. Sterling looked out the windows noticing that the black Suburbans were following them in reverse, they were staying in formation as well, they had the rear doors open, and men were firing at something behind them. A second large explosion rocked the bridge and this time Marty got a look at what had blown up.

"Holy shit! A Fed Ex truck just blew through the police checkpoint, men came out firing and the truck blew up on the bridge taking out the approach. Fuck, I think we're trapped!" Marty shouted. The gunfire was intense when Marty noticed large caliber rounds coming in from the front and back and numerous RPG rounds were hitting the escort vehicles causing fires. "Oh, my God! They have rockets and some heavy guns," Marty said to his father. The Secret Service agents shouted for them to stay in the limo, assuring them they would be safe as more rockets slammed into the vehicles around them killing the agents trying to fight back. One rocket entered the back window of one of the Suburbans that an agent was shooting from killing them all inside. Sterling was a smart man and looked at his son and calmly said,

"We are going to die today Marty. Let's be sure we do it with our dignity." Marty looked at his father and shook his head,

"Bullshit! I am not dying, not without a fight, I am not!"

Chapter 28.

Aug 4th. Davidsonville, Maryland.

   Local police were the first to show up at the CIG facility and the responding officers were blown away with the amount of bodies that were lying about. Several ambulances were arriving to take care of the wounded employees. Eight CIG employees had been killed during the attack and a dozen were wounded. One of the Little Bird pilots had flown two people to the nearest hospital and Paul could hear him landing having already returned. The two lawyers who owned CIG sat back and were visibly upset, both had spent their Navy careers behind desks never being shot at, but Paul could tell it was the loss of their employees that was bothering them. Both of the Directors were on their phones in the board room trying to get the ball rolling on the inevitable shit storm that was coming later this day.

   Paul and Thomas, along with Tim trailing behind them, walked into the board room. Paul had changed his clothes, his others were covered with Kelly's blood. Plus they were still the tiger striped MLB camo. He did not want the local cops thinking he was one of the bad guys laying dead outside. Tim had taken him into the armory and gotten him some fresh all black CIG military fatigues, and he was even able to grab a quick hot shower.

   A news helicopter had shown up very quickly and hovered above them. Thomas walked over to the video screen on the wall wondering if they were on the news already. Before Thomas had the TV turned on, Bryant was yelling on his phone and stood up, panic was setting in fast. He yelled for Thomas to turn on the TV, which he did. On every channel, there was video footage of men running through the streets of downtown Washington DC, shooting people indiscriminately.

The news was very fresh, and the report had little information, but said hundreds of eye witness accounts were coming from all over the city, roadblocks were holding traffic up, and car bomb detonations had occurred. She stated that there were reports of heavy weapons being used by the unknown attackers and it was confirmed the White House and Capital Hill were both under attack. A small segment of video of the violence showed the attackers wearing the tiger stripped camo fatigues. Paul dropped into a chair feeling sick,
"I failed," he said.

"No!" Thomas said, "I never should have gone to Zurich with Reese and gotten my picture taken. It is my fault," he added. Tim stood looking at the TV and shouted making sure everyone in the room could hear him,

"Hey, who gives a shit who's fault it is! That does not matter now! What does matter, is the assholes running around Washington shooting all those people! We have an armed unit ready to go. Let's fire up the Little Birds and go to town and shoot some fucking bad guys!" Thomas looked at Tim, then to Paul, and there was silence for a second until Thomas set the remote on the table and they all began walking out of the room. Bryant stepped in his way stopping them from leaving the room,

"I can not give you authorization for this action. You are civilians, not service personal." Bryant said but then added,
"But I will not stop you either. Stay in touch with us here and I will try and help coordinate." The three men said nothing and just ran out. Tim slapped Bryant on the shoulder as he passed him on the way out of the room. Tim radioed all his men to rearm immediately and informed them of the situation. Thomas and Paul retrieved arms from the armoury and loaded up tac vests with flash bangs and grenades.

Paul decided for the standard M-4 with the underslung M203 40mm grenade launcher, complete with a M68 close combat optic. Thomas took an Mk-16 Scar-L with holographic site and both men took extra ammo. Paul could hear the Little Birds spinning up outside already. The lawyers stood back watching on, feeling proud of their men, but clearly NOT wanting to come. Paul and the team headed for the helo pad, and Paul stopped to readjust the ballistic helmet straps of his tactical helmet. Suddenly Reese was beside him,

"No! I don't want to you to go. You're already hurt and you can't fight," she said concerned. Paul placed the helmet on his head and hooked the straps together.

"I have to," he said to her, and tears filled her eyes,

"Paul you're hurt, you can't go!" she yelled at him.

"Go to the board room. I will see you tonight," he kissed her on the cheek saying, "This is what we do," then ran and climbed on the Little Bird's outer deployment bench. Tim was waiting for Thomas and Paul to climb aboard and keyed his mic,

"This is the fun stuff boys," and then reached over and slapped the pilot's door and keyed his mic again. "Let's go!" and the four Little Birds lifted off as though they were being flown by one pilot, and immediately took a heading at full speed that would take them directly to Capital Hill.

As Paul sat on the crew bench of the Little Bird he felt so alive, he had missed this and knew this was where he belonged. Sitting on the side of a Bird skipping along the nap of the earth with a team of highly trained killers. The pilots kept the Birds low to the ground and moving fast, it was only minutes before they hit the outskirts of the city. Paul looked down seeing traffic jams and panicked citizens trying to leave the city. He looked forward at the smoke that was rising thick and black from numerous positions around the downtown area, as fires burned hot everywhere. The closer they got to downtown the signs of the anarchy were evident everywhere.

A blue and white police Air Bus AS 350 helicopter was hovering over Capital Hill making himself the perfect target as a SWAT sniper was trying to take a bead on someone down below. He was much too high and the CLG pilot tried to radio him a warning but was too late. When a shoulder fired surface to air missile detonated directly beside him, the pilot did what he could but began to spin out of control and crashed on Independence Ave. Paul watched as an MLB member ran to the chopper, firing inside making sure they were dead. Tim, not wasting a second, lifted his MK11 and looked through the Leopold site and fired one round hitting the murdering prick in the stomach. Paul watched as the man lay on the street holding his abdomen and kicking his legs in pain. Then Paul looked at Tim, who was clearly angry and wondered if he, one of the finest shots in the world, had gut shot the man on purpose.

Numerous car and truck bombs had been detonated throughout the downtown area, fires and destruction were everywhere. Thomas spoke into the radio telling all members of the team that there was a large concentration of MLB on the street in front of the Library of Congress in a shootout with the Capital Hill security forces and local police. Tim told the pilots to make a fast pass over the MLB from south to north. As they made the high-speed pass over the street every CIG member fired into the MLB, who were using the traffic jam as cover. This gave the local police a moment of relief as the MLB returned fire at the

Little Birds, who quickly left their line of sight as fast as they came in.

Paul waved to Tim, then pointed to the Library of Congress's rooftop. Tim, recognizing exactly what Paul meant, then ordered the Little Birds to offload one four-man team to the roof and the other team was led by Cyril to the back of the building on the ground to move inside and take positions from windows. This would allow the MLB to be stuck between the CIG operatives and the local security defending Capital Hill. These actions were done without hesitation. The now empty, unarmed Little Bird began flying around at high speeds trying to draw fire from the ground hoping to take enemy attention off civilians.

The outside channel came to life as the situation room at the CIG headquarters began contacting them. It was Director Bryant's voice,

"Central Station to Snatch One." Tim immediately answered,

"Snatch one, go!"

"Central Station, all friendly forces informed that you are now friendly. Friendly military assets came under heavy ambush and are being held up but are making ground. Request from Secret Service you go immediately to Arlington Memorial Bridge to assist in high value extraction, over." Bryant explained. Tim replied,

"Snatch One, roger, must advise, Snatch Two deployed to Library of Congress, Snatch One on route. Request information on high value target over." The pilots and team members had been listening and without any orders from Tim, the two Little Bird's pilots flew along the ground in and out of the trees, buildings, and monuments to the designated bridge. Central Station had not replied, but once they hit the air space over the Potomac River there was no need for them to say anything else. They could all see the President's limousine on the bridge being shot to pieces and defending it there were only a few remaining Secret Service agents left. Both sides of the bridge had been blown out and MLB had vehicles lined up and were using them for cover. The MLB were firing from the east side of the river into the motorcade with what he suspected was a fifty-caliber Browning, belt fed heaving machine gun from the back of a parcel delivery truck. Tim counted at least twenty MLB on the east side, and another twenty or more on the west.

Tim acknowledged the request and told the pilots make some passes and thin out the herd on the east side of the Potomac. After this was done the two empty Birds arrived in the area and continued their harassment. One of the pilots was in contact with an F-15 that arrived flying over watch and asked it for a few flyovers, which the pilot happily provided.

During this confusion, the team flew to the east side of the river to the Arlington Cemetery Metro Station and offloaded out of sight on the tracks just before a highway overpass. Tim ordered two members to stay on the helos to provide support from the air. Thomas, Tim and Paul along with three other operators began moving east to the bridge. After a few minutes of running they were in a small group of trees beside the road overlooking a traffic circle filled with abandoned cars and well armed MLB members. Paul watched as some civilians were standing back watching what was happening.

Paul and Thomas commented on how they could hear the MLB laughing as they fired into the trapped motorcade.

"Damn, we need a tank," Tim whispered. Paul examined the MLB in their position and replied,

"No, that would make things too easy." Then Paul lifted his M203 and fired a 40mm grenade into the center of the MLB position. It exploded killing two members right away and caused two cars to catch fire. The MLB did not know where the incoming fire had come from. They were too busy shooting and laughing at the motorcade not paying any attention to the area around them. Tim lifted his MK11, deployed the swivel base bi-pod and took aim as he laid prone on the ground. An MLB member was looking around showing just a little too much head, allowed Tim to squeeze the trigger hitting him in the forehead, spraying the man beside him with brain matter. That man stood up in shock looking at his friend, Tim wsted no time and placed a round in his forehead the same as he did to his friend's. The team sat still letting Tim do his job, ten shots and ten kills until no MLB member in the group was willing to lift their head for fear of literally losing it. Paul took another 40mm grenade and dropped it into the group of vehicles, and a second later they could hear men screaming.

Soon two police officers and a small group of civilians came out of the Metro Station and ran up behind them and were stopped by a team member. The two police officers began to argue that they wanted to help. Thomas returned to talk to them and after a minute reluctantly they agreed to stay back. Tim fired another shot into the position killing another MLB member who found the courage to lift his head for a look.

"Shit Paul, I thought you were training these guys, it is a god damn turkey shoot!" Paul said nothing in return to Tim.

"Okay they have had enough, let's move on them," Tim said, then called his men to attention and lined them up. "They won't come out, so we go in. Use the cars for cover." Tim pointed to the police who were standing back. "You two bring up the rear and stay low!" The two policemen nodded, and Tim pointed forward. They began moving slowly on the MLB position, there had to be at least ten to fifteen left by Paul estimate, but none were visible. Then two stood up and opened fire at the advancing team who stopped amongst some cars and dropped down. A short firefight began and as the MLB fired at Tim, Thomas and Paul the other team members moved around to the left out of sight behind the cars. Then at the same time, they stood and fired into the three MLB fighters, killing all three, Paul had stood and gotten two more. Thomas pulled out a frag grenade, pulled the pin, waited a two count and threw it into the area they suspected the rest of the MLB to be hiding. The grenade went off and another man was screaming in pain. Tim waved for the two police officers to come up and began yelling orders for the remaining MLB to come out. It only took a few seconds before the remaining fighters held their hands up and stood. They were quickly directed into the middle of the traffic circle and told to lay flat on the grass. Their weapons were gathered, and Tim drafted a few civilians to assist the two cops, and armed them with MLB weapons,

"If they move, pop them!" He said to the newly drafted civilians as they nervously held the assault rifles.

The time from offloading from the Little Birds until this point had only been around five minutes but seemed much longer to Paul as their attention went back to the President as the .50 Cal could still be heard banging away short bursts into the motorcade. There was a lot more gunfire coming from the city now as well. It sounded like the reaction forces were breaking in now. Paul and the team left the two cops and civilians in charge of the thirteen prisoners and headed quickly to the bridge. The CIG Little Birds were still harassing the

MLB on the far side of the river and more than once had taken some rocket fire.

They were now on the western side of the bridge, a large explosion had taken a piece of it down, but they were still able to walk on the right side. Tim keyed his radio,
"Snatch One to Central Station, we are entering the bridge, request confirmation Secret Service was informed, good guys coming onto bridge from west, over." A moment later they had confirmation and they began sprinting to the motorcade that was more than halfway across the river.

Once they arrived at the Presidential limousine they had a challenging time getting to it. Out of the twelve vehicles in the motorcade seven were on fire. Paul reached the limo finding the back door open and the vehicle empty. He kept his body low and moved to the front of the limousine looking for President Hunton, who he found at the front of the motorcade with a M-4 in his hands firing at eastern bank. His son Marty was nearby with a rifle as well but was helping a wounded Secret Service agent who was bleeding badly from his leg. The .50 Cal must have noticed an increase in movement as the incoming fire increased.

"Mr. President, sir. You must come with us!" Paul yelled. The heavy rounds slammed into the armored vehicles all around them again causing everyone to lie flat on the ground, then two more rockets hit the front vehicles causing more devastation. "Sir, we must go!" Paul yelled. Marty

crawled to his father, he had taken off his dress blue coat and had placed on a Kevlar vest, the President was wearing one as well. Sterling ignored Paul again and fired another burst at
the bank. Paul was getting angry and for the third time Paul yelled, "Sir!" and grabbed him by the shoulder and began dragging him away,
"Let me go!" Sterling yelled at Paul and jerked his arm loose, "I can move myself!" He shouted as he loaded a fresh mag into the M-4.
   Marty crawled over beside him,
"We are not going anyplace until that 50 is silenced," Marty shouted.
"Yea, working on that," Paul replied. Thomas had found a good spot and was firing at the eastern bank. Paul keyed his radio,
"Hey Tim, that .50 is making to much noise, buddy!"
"I am trying, they got a sniper on the Lincoln memorial that needs to be taken out first. One minute." Tim was trying to find a vantage point so he could take out the sniper without getting killed himself. It took him a minute, but he climbed inside a burning Secret Service vehicle and lay himself on the front seat. He could see just the top foot of the Lincoln memorial and the sniper was scanning the mess on the bridge,
   "That bastard is the one that killed most of my men," President Hunton said. Tim placed the crosshairs on the sniper's forehead, adjusted for the wind and squeezed the trigger. The MLB sniper

never moved an inch, but his rifle fell off to the ground.

"Got him! Case of bear Mr. :President." Tim shouted then quickly repositioned himself and jumped up placing the rifle on the hood of another truck and looked for the .50 Cal, it had been firing at them from a back of a parcel delivery truck. Tim was exposed but it only took a second for him to fire, hitting the machine gunner in the chest, he then quickly fired two more shots into the weapon itself taking it out of action, then dropped back down. Paul threw a smoke grenade over the vehicles, waited for the smoke to spread out and took the President by the arm and they started running for the west bank. Thomas and Tim followed with Marty and the last remaining healthy Secret Service agent. Tim told his remaining three men to stay on the bridge and help the wounded Secret service men.

Once they got back across the bridge Tim called the Little Birds in for extraction. The birds came in fast, President Hunton was thrown onto the exterior bench with his last Secret Service agent, and his son and Tim climbed on the other side and the pilot took off followed by the two Birds that had the teammates providing support.

One of the empty Birds picked up Paul and Thomas. Paul wondered if they should be on this one helicopter. It had taken so much rifle fire he was not sure it was going to stay aloft. They left the area fast heading to the river as low as possible, then after getting out of the city they circled around and began returning to the CIG facility. A news helicopter appeared and was following them. It came up close beside them with a cameraman in the back filming them. Paul raised his rifle to the ready making sure that it was camera and not a weapon the man held. The cameraman zoomed in on President Hunton sitting on the side of the helicopter still holding the rifle. Then it swung up and over capturing video of his son on the other side covered in blood and holding a rifle as well. Tim keyed his radio.

"Snatch One to Central Station, coming home with VIP and junior, and if you don't believe me check CNN."

Chapter 29.

Aug 4th. Davidsonville, Maryland

Paul walked the President up to the boardroom where both directors were impatiently waiting for him. His last Secret Service agent not more than two feet behind him looked shell shocked and emotional and was on the phone calling for reinforcements to their location. Thomas was trying to tell him they would be fine here, but he refused to listen.

The second CIG strike team who was not present earlier that morning was now starting to arrive onsite and were already gearing up, eager to get into the fight. Cromwell and Bryant introduced Paul, Reese and Thomas to President Sterling. They started at the beginning telling the entire story all the way through right to the point of meeting him on the bridge. Sterling let them finish the story and was almost in disbelief. He asked them to again to tell him about Martin Sibley making sure he got all the details about his soon to be former Secretary of Defense.

"I thought he was my friend," Sterling said sadly then became angry, "Bryant, find Martin today! I want him placed under arrest today!" Then he turned to the CIA Director, "Cromwell, I want the evidence linking the Russians to this as soon as possible! I want it concrete, and I want it soon!" President Sterling was trying to calm himself down and walked over to the TV screen watching the news footage. He turned up the volume and listened to the female reporter updating the nation. She reported,

"Large amounts of this unknown group have been surrendering to police and emergency forces. Apparently, many refused to fight and chose to hide and wait out the turmoil. Still hundreds of their fellow group members decided to attack and many are still determined to fight on." Sterling turned down the volume again,

"I want this to end! I want every one of these people arrested or shot!" he shouted as he pointed at the screen. Then he seemed to calm down and calmly said, "I need to address the nation."

Marty walked into the boardroom still holding his rifle, like a true Marine his father thought looking at him.

"Dad, I am going back into the city, the CIG team leader O'Brien is going back out, they have men in the city and I am going in with them to help them out," Marty said to his father. Sterling, being a former Marine himself, knew what his son was feeling and felt it himself. He also knew his son would probably not forgive him if he ordered him to stay and simply said,

"Be careful." Paul was feeling useless sitting in the boardroom and stood up out of his chair,

"I will be going to," Paul said as Reese rolled her eyes. Just then the sound of helicopters could be heard rumbling outside. Not the Little Birds or the news chopper, but large ones and a lot of them. Thomas walked to the window and looked out,

"The Marines are here for you sir." Thomas said addressing the President.

Marty and Paul walked out of the room and headed to the armory to reload. Tim was waiting with several members of CIG's second team as they loaded up.

"Paul, are you coming?" he asked.

"Damn right," Paul replied, and Tim gave him a thumb up,

"Good, we are heading to Capital Park; Cyril and Snatch Two have been in it bad a few times with some MLB. They have chased them into the ball park, they need more men to round them up. Local police and military are in the area, but he said it is just a cluster down there."

They climbed back on the Little Birds and took off as soon as the Marines had landed. They headed back into the city the same way they had come in, low and fast. It was just like the way they had done that morning and it only took a few minutes. One difference this time was the amount of aircraft in the air. Fighter jets zipped around like bees and dozens of Blackhawks were dropping troops in all over the place. There were hundreds of fires burning, many government buildings were a total loss, and in several parts of the city Paul could see the bodies of hundreds of dead civilians lying in the streets.

Tim was in constant contact with Cyril, who directed them to land in the south parking lot of Capital Park. They quickly disembarked the birds and set them back up and they began scouting the stadium from above. Cyril walked up to Tim. The noise of the planes and helicopters covering the city was loud making Cyril yell for Tim to hear,

"Hey, congratulations on the big rescue you guys got today, yea as you guys were trying to get famous, we have been here killing evil." Cyril teased Tim. Tim grinned at him and asked,

"What you got?" Cyril pointed to the ball park and began briefing, "I have at least twenty in here. We chased them inside, a bad crew Tim, I saw them killing all the Black people like it was sport. I want them bad, really bad."

"Alright then," Tim agreed and called a Little Bird in for him and a spotter to be flown to the roof to provide cover.

Once Tim was positioned above, the team went to the front doors. The MLB had left a door lying on the ground when they entered the ball park, so breaching was easy. Cyril entered first, and took his team left, while Paul took his team with Marty to the right and they began walking slow clearing each corner and room as they went. They found the concession stands hard to clear as the counters made good cover to hide behind. Gunfire came from behind them as Cyril's team engaged someone and it came over the net,
"Bad guy down."

Paul lead his team slowly down the long corridor filled with food and memorabilia stations very slowly. Tim's voice came over the net,

"Bad guy down on second base."

Paul could see the men's washroom ahead and began moving to the door. As he got closer, a man wearing the MLB uniform poked his head out and raised a rifle. Paul, having been advancing with his rifle at his shoulder, quickly aimed and shot the man in the chest. As soon as the man hit the floor at least five others began firing at Paul and his team.

Paul dove behind a hotdog stand and found Marty already there, and they began to return fire. The MLB fired wildly at them and Paul realized that neither side was going to win this fight until better positions could be taken. Bullets tore the hotdog stand apart and Marty was covered in mustard as a large container exploded beside him after being struck by a bullet. Paul raised up and fired a burst then dropped down. Then jumped up again and fired another burst killing the man he aimed at. He fired another burst then jumped over the counter and ran to the bathroom he was moving towards earlier. Paul quickly ran through the door stepping over the MLB member he had shot in the face minutes earlier and moved through the bathroom clearing it as he went and found it empty. He then started back to the door as it gave a good vantage point on several other attacker's positions involved in the fight. As he moved near the door someone opened up with a rifle on full auto firing through the door as he ran into the bathroom screaming at the top of his lungs shooting until his weapon was empty. Paul was forced to jump back before getting hit by this wild spray, and as he jumped backwards he fell flat on his back and the man running dropped his empty rifle and dove on top of him.

It was several seconds before Paul realized it was Jones he was rolling on the ground with, who pulled out a knife and brought it down hard but struck one of the full magazines in Paul's tactical vest. Jones brought the knife back up and tried again, and Paul managed to get a good grip on his wrist and held his hand away from his body. Jones began punching Paul with his other hand many times over in the head and face. Paul pushed Jones away causing him to fall back and both men rolled over and stood up. The second Jones got to his feet he was coming at Paul again screaming, "Traitor!" as he swung the knife wildly. Paul moved back and tried pulling out his pistol. Jones seeing this swung the knife at Paul's hand striking flesh and slicing it open, knocking the gun loose and it fell to the ground. Paul moved away, and Jones rushed him. Paul pulled out his bayonet and both men slashed at each other trying to see who would draw blood first. Jones won as he slashed Paul's right forearm open causing Paul to lose his knife. Paul was good at a lot of things, but knife fighting was a weak area for him.

Jones rushed at Paul again swinging his knife and screaming, "Die! Die! Fucking die!" Paul moved away and struck Jones in the face with a straight left hand making him stumble away and shook his head and shouted, "Goddamn traitor, I am going to enjoy killing you!" Paul, having had enough of Jones's mouth a long time ago yelled back,

"Oh, God, shut up already you fucking hillbilly!" Jones's face filled with even more rage as he started coming at Paul again just as Marty ran into the room with his rifle at his shoulder and fired a long burst into Jones, killing him instantly.

"Are you okay?" Marty asked as he pulled out a field dressing for Paul's arm and hand as they were bleeding badly. Paul nodded to Marty,

"Thank you buddy, the sound of his voice was killing me!" Marty smiled and said,

"Funny, I thought it was the knife that was going to kill you." Marty finished the dressing on Paul then retrieved his weapons from the floor. The fighting had moved down deeper into the stadium. By the time Paul and Marty had caught up to the team, the shooting had stopped. They cleared the entire stadium and to be sure they swept it again, which took them hours then they all met outside and turned the building over to some army troops holding the streets.

They had been inside the stadium for hours and all non-law enforcement and non-military units were being told to leave the streets as there were thousands of troops pouring into the Capital from all over. There was still some shooting being heard to the north and buildings were still burning. Tim called in the Birds and pulled them all out. As they flew back Paul watched the air space over Washington where hundreds of helicopters were still dropping off troops and carrying the wounded out. Paul looked down at the open areas around the Washington Monument, the entire area was being outfitted with hospital tents and ambulances were coming in with their lights flashing and sirens blowing. Paul was glad to be getting out of the city, he was tired and needed rest and food.

The flight back was slow and uneventful and when they had arrived, the President and the Marines had gone. Reese and both Directors had left with the President. A mountain of food had been brought in for everyone at the facility. The police were still there trying to preserve the crime scene, so everyone had retreated to the armory and combat preparation hanger, where they ate chicken and pasta and drank a ton of cold beer. A CIG medic had stitched up Paul's arm and hand for him and the beer was helping with the pain.

Paul finished eating and walked outside, it was dark now and he looked up to the moon. He could hear fighter planes flying overhead as they circled the city. Tim came walking out of the hanger and handed Paul a fresh cold beer.

"Here buddy," he said as he handed him a cold one.

"Thanks Tim," Paul said as he opened it and took a long drink. Tim placed his hand on Paul's shoulder getting his attention,

"I was just talking to Thomas, and the lawyers are planning to offer you a job."

"Really?" Paul said surprised.

"Yes, I want you on my team, Paul." Tim said or more asked. Paul was smiling, "Dude, I was hoping for this, but what about my back?" Paul asked concerned. Tim smiled,

"Dude, look what you have done the past few months with your broken back. I and they think you are fine." Paul opened his fresh cold beer and felt like a new man. Tim looked at the bandages on his arm and hand, "You okay buddy?" he asked concerned.

"Sure, it hurts a bit, not like the raging pain in my nose, face, ribs, and abdomen. I was tortured, you know? But my back feels okay though," Paul said smiling at Tim,

"Fucking puss!" Tim said back laughing at him and the two stood outside in the cool night air drinking some beer and listening to the planes and helicopters when Thomas joined them carrying a bucket of ice water and beer. Moments before Thomas was watching TV and informed his friends on what he had heard. The news had said the only fighting left was in the north of the city in two separate pockets. He said that President Sterling had spoken to the nation and explained to the people what had happened and exposed the Russian and Cartel connections. He exposed Martin Sibley and Allan Costner as well, stating they were missing and asked the nation to report their locations if known. He told everyone about Isaack and what he wanted to do. Thomas explained all of this and told Paul it was replaying if he wanted to see it. He simply shook his head,

"No." Paul had asked if there had been any problems in other parts of the nation like Isaack had planned for and Thomas shrugged his shoulders.

Paul's phone rang in his pocket and he pulled it out, he was hoping it was Reese, but it was an unknown number displayed, He knew instantly who it was and Paul felt sick as he answered the call,

"Hello Paul Totten," Isaack's voice was clear as day,

"Isaack," Paul replied. Tim and Thomas both crowded around Paul to hear, Paul placed the phone on speaker so they could listen,

"I saw you on the news rescuing the President. You're a real hero, Paul," Isaack said sarcastically.

"I would have assumed you would have died fighting like your fucked up followers!" Paul sarcastically taunted back, and Isaack seemed to take the bait.

"I would kill your family if you had any Paul. You're still all alone Paul and it will be that way the rest of your life! Your father died with a disappointment for a son," Isaack yelled into the phone. Thomas placed his hand on Paul's shoulder letting him know he was not alone. Tim reached down and grabbed his groin and held his middle finger to the phone. These two small ridiculous small acts made Paul feel good and brought a grin to his face.

"Isaack, I want you to know that wherever you go on this planet we will find you, and whatever dark place you crawl into and go to sleep, when you wake, I will be there, and I will end you, like I ended Alfred, and Jones." Paul was expecting Isaack to freak on the phone, but he said nothing, and the phone went dead.

"Wow, I expected something more from him," Thomas stated.

"Yea, me too, fuck that douchebag!" Tim said, reaching into the bucket of ice water and pulling out more beers for everyone.

Chapter 30.

August 10th. Washington DC.

 Paul stood in a fine suit at the Carleton Ritz in Washington D.C, Reese had helped him pick it out the morning before, then helped him off the floor when he found out the price came to almost a grand. She insisted he be dressed in a fine suit for today the President of the United States himself had earlier addressed the nation after the attack from the MLB had devastated Washington. Now this evening President Hunton was hosting a dinner party for the men who had saved him and his son and the numerous other people that were instrumental in stopping the horrific events that had shocked the nation.

 During his speech earlier in the day, he spoke of the terrific losses the nation suffered nine days prior. Even though Isaack's plan of uniting and inspiring the many militia groups around the nation had failed and only three other groups around the country took up arms totaling seventeen people, not the thousands that Isaack had predicated. There were still over three thousand civilians killed, two hundred twenty-two police and security forces and ninety-six military personnel. The numbers would have been much higher except the MLB were not prepared for so many civilians to join the fight against them, giving the much-needed time until the military had arrived. Isaack had brought over nine hundred people to Washington, but then more than four hundred gave up without firing a shot.

Six days ago, Martin Sibley and Allan Costner were arrested in Canada trying to sneak aboard a freighter heading for east Africa, with them a number of Canadian dock workers that had been working for Isaack for years removing cargo and bypassing any inspections. Reese and Bryant flew to Canada with a team the next day to interview them. Costner refused to say a word even with the threat of the death penalty. Martin was different, he turned on everyone at once with a hint of a possible deal, giving up everything on his childhood friend, Isaack. He even went so far as giving everything on the Russians even down to when Boris had turned him years prior in Moscow after finding proof of a homosexual relationship. He told them that Shura Osetsky had arranged transport for all of them out of the country at the request of Boris and that they would all meet somewhere in Turkey but had not been told where.

After President Hunton had given his speech praising the responders and emergency personnel and the dinner following, he had both directors, Thomas, Tim, Paul, Reese, both CIG owners, Marty and his wife with a few dozen others to meet him in the hotel lobby bar that had been closed to the public for drinks. Paul was sitting with Tim drinking Irish whisky on ice laughing at Reese as she choked on a shot of tequila that Thomas had given her. The lobby bar was dark with high-backed leather booths surrounding the outside and had a grand piano off to the side, it was basically what you would expect in a high-end luxury hotel. Thomas came over and sat down with another round for the three of them. Sterling was talking to Bryant and Cromwell at the bar about the upcoming NCAA football season arguing with Cromwell that Army this year would be the team of the century.

Marty sat at the piano talking to his mother and one of her aides who seemed to be in awe of the young Marine who was dressed in his blues. Paul was watching Reese as she walked over to listen to the President talking about the Yale football team, then turned to Reese and her USC background. Cromwell left the group smiling and walked over to the three and sat down.

"Boys," the director of the CIA casually said and the three nodded to him and raised their glasses. Then Cromwell looked around making sure no one was listening, Paul thought he was going to tell them something sensitive when he asked, "Have you guys ever thought of working for me?" The three never had time to answer when the two lawyers appeared from out of nowhere like ninjas making sure Cromwell was not going to steal their star employees, even though Paul had not had an offer of employment from CIG.

The three began laughing hard, the free drinks were starting to take effect. Reese walked over and sat down on Paul's lap kissing him on the cheek. He had been staying at her apartment with her and was enjoying it, even though she had hardly been around due to working almost sixteen hours a day since the attack.

It was then when Paul's phone rang, it was sitting on the table and everyone looked at Paul to answer it. "Unknown number," Paul read on the screen and started getting a bad feeling but was trying to disbelieve that Isaack and would try calling again.

"Hello," Paul said answering and he waited for a reply.

"Hello, Paul Totten." Isaack's voice said calmly, Paul dropped his head down and began shaking it back and forth as he instantly became angry.

"What the fuck do you want Isaack?" Paul shouted into the phone, and Cromwell immediately took his own phone out of his pocket and began dialing. Paul readjusted in his chair as Isaack began taunting him again.

"Paul, I saw you on TV standing beside the President today. Good for you son," Isaack stated calmly, and Paul heard a familiar snap on Isaack's end of the line and Paul realized that he was lighting a cigarette. Isaack exhaled into the phone and started talking again. "I want you to know Paul, I like it here where I am at these days, it is a little hotter than I am used to but, I will get used it." Paul felt the rage flow through his body,

"What do you want Isaack?" And then there was a long pause.

"I just wanted you to know I was thinking about you," he said, and the phone went dead. Paul set the phone down on the table and took his drink and sipped the cold whiskey. Cromwell was still on his phone and after a minute he placed his phone into his pocket and looked at Paul and smiling.

"My people traced the call, he is somewhere in Turkey," then his smile turned to a grin. "We will find him."

President Hunton walked over to the crowd around Paul's table and asked what was going on as the mood was quiet. Paul explained to him about his recent call, he then looked at Cromwell expecting an answer but never got one. Paul looked at Sterling and asked him to sit, which he did. Paul nervously began speaking to him,

"Sir, I have a favor to ask, sir."

"Anything." Sterling confidently said, Paul took a drink finishing his whiskey and called the waiter for another.

"Mr. Cromwell is confident he can find Isaack in Turkey, and when he does, sir... Can you send us in to get him?" Sterling thought for a moment and then looked at Cromwell who simply shrugged back at him.

"Well, I guess so, but no risks. If he is highly guarded just call in a drone strike and kill the bastard."

Chapter 31.

Sept 21. Sirnak, Turkey. Near the Iraq boarder.

It was past two am local time, Paul crawled on his belly keeping his body as low as possible to the ground, then he slowly looked over the old stone wall at the house and stables below. CIA drone operators had watched Isaack enter this house earlier this day and had only seen him come out to smoke cigarettes and he had not left the premises. Intel said he had three body guards and the owner of the property was suspected to be on the payroll of Shura Osetsky, who unfortunately was not present at this moment. Thomas was beside him staying down out of sight. Tim and Cyril were up higher on the hill looking down on them through the optics of Tim's rifle and everyone felt better knowing Tim was on over watch.

They had communications this night, not with the CIG board room but with Langley. Director Cromwell and President Hunton were present along with Reese and the two lawyers. The President had given specific orders if possible to try and take Isaack alive, but only if it could be done with out high risk to themselves.

"Snatch One to Home Plate," Tim said over the satellite radio and waited for Langley to respond.

"Home Plate to Snatch One, send." came back clear through his earpiece.

"Rodger moving towards Marlboro man's position, over." The eight-man team began slowly moving closer. Paul had been the one to select

Isaack's codename Marlboro man, he felt it fitted for the insane amount the man smoked.

They moved slow getting constant updates from Langley as they watched a constant feed from the drone high above. At two hundred yards Tim went prone again with his silenced M110 SASS and deployed the BI-pod and told the team to hold. In the dim light around the stables he saw movement. Through his optic, he clearly saw a dog, ears up looking in their direction. He knew the dog would start barking any second, he placed the cross hairs on the dog's head and squeezed the trigger, the weapon's silencer muffled the shot and a fraction of a second later the bullet struck the dog making it fall backwards dead without making a sound. Tim waited an entire minute looking for any more signs of movement and none was seen. He calculated the situation then ordered his team to move forward.

Paul and Thomas were in front of an old four-foot-high stone wall that carried itself all the way around the house and stables. Paul took a good look at the old mud brick house and guessed it was two hundred years old at least, the tin roof he suspected was much newer along with the satellite dish and electric lights. There were two vehicles in the yard, one a light blue four door Jeep that Isaack had arrived in earlier and a like new silver Nissan Titan truck.

The team had moved into position surrounding the property when the front door of the house opened and a man wearing a black leather jacket and grey pants walked out carrying an older M-16 rifle he had slung over his shoulder. Every man dropped out of sight and the guard began calling his dog. He had called several times and clearly became suspicious and began searching for it when it never came running to his call.

"Damn it!" Paul whispered to himself, they should have moved the dead dog. The guard walked the perimeter of his house and saw his dog near the stable. He must have assumed the dog was sleeping as he calmly walked up to it. Paul readied his silenced H&K MK 23 pistol and quickly stood and fired two quick shots that both struck the man in the head and he dropped silently to the ground. The team instantly moved over the old stone wall and took positions around the house. Tim quickly made his way down and stacked up at the front door with Paul and Thomas. Paul, holding his silenced pistol in front of him, slowly opened the door and walked inside. The house was dimly lit and hot inside, the interior of the house was finely furnished with clean rugs and posh furniture and filled with electronics like TVs and laptops. One of the bodyguards was sleeping on the couch. This man was not Turkish, he had a real Eastern Europe look about him and Paul thought it must be one of Shura's men. It never mattered because Cyril silently walked over and cupped the mans mouth and slammed his knife deep into his skull before he could make a sound. They made their way down the hallway and there were two closed doors. Tim and Cyril stacked on the one on the right while Paul and Thomas stacked on the left door. They opened the doors at the same time and walked in. Paul looked at Isaack sleeping peacefully alone, there was an old model ten Smith and Wesson .38 on the stand beside the bed, Thomas quietly picked it up. In the other room Tim and Cyril saw two men sleeping on bunk style beds, while for some strange reason Paul picked up Isaack's lighter and quietly placed it in his pocket.

Isaack was suddenly awakened by a thudding sound as Tim and Cyril ended the two sleeping men's lives in the next bedroom. Isaack fought to get his eyes and body working when he noticed his bedroom door was open and saw someone sitting in the chair beside the bed and another armed man standing beside him. He looked at the two men with black painted faces and all black battledress and horror filled his face when he realized the one in the chair was Paul. Isaack tried going for the revolver he had left on the stand, but it was gone. Paul leaned forward and slowly stood, then slowly walked over close to the bed and coldly said,

"I told you Isaack, that you would wake up and I would be here." Then he raised his pistol to Isaack's forehead, Isaack looked at Paul and quietly said,

"Hello Paul Tot..." Isaack's greeting was cut off when Paul quickly squeezed the trigger.

Chapter 32.

Sept 26. Washington DC.

Paul sat in the little deli not too far down the street from the FBI headquarters waiting for Reese who he could see walking down the street meeting him for lunch. He had already ordered her a bowl of clam chowder and an iced tea. Paul sat back in his chair happy when he saw her coming and again thanked god for bringing her into his life and giving him something to look forward to every day. The old deli he waited in had just reopened as most of the city was finally getting back to some portion of a normal routine, even though there were still some armed troops patrolling the streets, but not as many as yesterday.

Reese walked in and he stood to greet her, she walked over and kissed him on the cheek smiling when she saw him waiting. She immediately sat down and took her spoon.

"I am starving," she said with a sigh as she took her first spoonful. Paul took a spoonful as well and it was good and nodded his head in approval. Reese had several more spoonfuls then wiped her mouth and asked Paul, "Well, did you take the job?" Paul smiled and said,

"Yes, the lawyers offered me a good deal. Cromwell offered me a job again this morning as well, but CIG is where I am suited for I think." Reese smiled and returned to her chowder. They kept talking as they ate laughing and enjoying their food. Reese finished most of her chowder then told Paul she had to get back to work and set the remaining portion of her soup in front of Paul, kissed him goodbye and left while Paul began eating her chowder. As he was cleaning out the bowl with a piece of bread an older man in his mid fifties walked up, pulled out the same chair Reese had been sitting in and sat down with Paul. Paul looked at the man wondering what the deal was. The older man then pointed at two other younger men sitting in the corner watching and Paul could tell with a glance the men were there for the stranger's protection. The strange man began speaking in a deep Russian accent,

"Do you know who I am?" Paul looked at the man and got a very bad feeling once he heard the Russian accent.

"No," Paul answered carefully.

"My name is Boris Donsky." Paul grabbed a napkin and wiped his mouth and answered,

"Yes, I have heard of you. Fucking prick!" Paul said with anger in his tone. Boris reached onto the table and took a bread stick from the center and took a bite, and as he chewed he began speaking again.

"You have deconstructed everything I have tried working on for the past four years," Boris stated coldly, and Paul glanced around the room and found the two men sitting in the corner watching the meeting closely. Paul returned his attention to Boris.

"There are troops right outside on the street," Paul stated letting Boris know help was only a second away if he needed any. Boris looked out the windows seeing the two-armed soldiers standing on the corner. "My men are not for you Mr. Totten, they are here for me and my safety from you." Paul smiled and placed a piece of the fresh bread in his mouth and stated,

"You were smart in doing so, if they were not here, I would have already busted your fuckin head open. Now comrade, what the hell do you want from me?" Boris placed both elbows on the table and leaned forward to Paul so to make sure he had Paul's complete attention.

"You have hurt me Paul, you and CIG have hurt me, my position in my country has been severely hurt. My relationship with President Shuisky has been severely damaged and he is not a man one should disappoint." Boris was visibly getting upset and slamming his hand on the table and shouted, "and it is your fault!" The people in the deli all stopped and looked at the irate Russian. As he calmed down, Paul silently sat and waited until the people returned to their lunches. Boris took a breath and began speaking again, "I understand you are entering the intelligence game and have taken a position with CIG." Paul said nothing. He sat silently and simply took a drink of his coffee. This seemed to irritate Boris, who needed to take a few additional deep breaths. "Paul, I want you to know, if you interfere with my operations again, I promise, you will die!" Paul listened to Boris make his threat and felt himself becoming angry and felt he needed to address this man's threat immediately.

"Listen, I have been offered a spot with CIG and will be checking into how you found that out so fast. You have made a promise to me, so I will make a promise back to you. This mess in my country was your doing, we know this as Sibley told us everything. I am holding you personally responsible for all these innocent people who died." Paul stood up and reached into his pocket and pulled out a small bundle of bills and dropped forty dollars on the table. He then leaned over and looked Boris dead in the eyes and coldly said, "If we do meet again, on that day, well, then that will be an interesting day." He said nothing else to Boris who sat looking indifferently at him. Paul then placed the remaining bills in his hand back in his pocket and gave the two body guards a cold look, then simply walked out of the deli onto the street and headed to his truck which was parked not far away. "Yes." He thought to himself, "That will be an interesting day."

THE END.

About the Author.

Dan Hopkins was born October 15, 1970 in Red Deer, Alberta, Canada where he lives with his wife Tania, daughter Erica and a new puppy Nash. Dan is a former Army Reservist and has been a Federal Corrections Officer in Canada for twenty years. After he began writing some years back as a hobby, he started to bring chapters to work for his friends and colleagues to read. Enjoying it, they convinced him to continue with the story and publish his first novel Third Law.

Made in the USA
San Bernardino, CA
04 January 2019